Inexcusable

PIECES

PIECES

CHRIS LYNCH

SIMON & SCHUSTER BFYR

New York   London   Toronto   Sydney   New Delhi

SIMON & SCHUSTER BFYR

An imprint of Simon & Schuster Children's Publishing Division
1230 Avenue of the Americas, New York, New York 10020

SIMON & SCHUSTER BFYR is a trademark of Simon & Schuster, Inc.
For information about special discounts for bulk purchases, please contact Simon & Schuster Special Sales at 1-866-506-1949 or business@simonandschuster.com.
The Simon & Schuster Speakers Bureau can bring authors to your live event. For more information or to book an event, contact the Simon & Schuster Speakers Bureau at 1-866-248-3049 or visit our website at www.simonspeakers.com.
Also available in a SIMON & SCHUSTER BFYR hardcover edition
Book design by Krista Vossen
The text for this book is set in Berling LT.
Manufactured in the United States of America
First SIMON & SCHUSTER BFYR paperback edition January 2014
2 4 6 8 10 9 7 5 3 1
The Library of Congress has cataloged the hardcover edition as follows:
Lynch, Chris, 1962–
Pieces / Chris Lynch.
p. cm.
Summary: Eighteen-year-old Eric deals with the loss of his older brother Duane by meeting three of the seven recipients of Duane's organs a year after his death, and pondering who they are to him, and he to them.
ISBN 978-1-4169-2703-7 (hardcover)
[1. Interpersonal relations—Fiction. 2. Brothers—Fiction. 3. Donation of organs, tissues, etc.—Fiction. 4. Death—Fiction. 5. Grief—Fiction.] I. Title.
PZ7.L979739Pie 2013
[Fic]—dc23
2011042049
ISBN 978-1-4424-5441-5 (paperback)
ISBN 978-1-4424-5311-1 (eBook)

PIECES

PHILOSOPHY

My brother is a philosopher. I know this because he's told me, countless times. More than just a philosopher, even.

"Philoso-raptor," he calls himself. "Swift of mind, rapaciously inquisitive." On his twentieth birthday this year he alerted me to the fact that "at approximately two dumps a day, more than seven hundred a year, times twenty years, that puts me over the fourteen-thousand mark for squatting, most of it on the toilet. That, my man, is a lot of contemplation."

That's my brother.

He's always telling me to be philosophical, to take things philosophically. I've never entirely wrapped my mind around what that means, but it seems right now is as good a time as there ever will be to figure that out.

There's a moss-green river that cuts in half just in time to bypass the hospital on both sides. Sometimes it doesn't appear green, but even at those times it smells green. Doesn't matter, though. People are always on the banks, walking up and down, sitting in the park that belongs half to the hospital, half to the river. Because of the sound. It's millions of splashy voices all going at once, and this river is never, ever silent.

I'm standing with my back to the voices and my front to the gleam of the new hospital wing rising up, eight stories of yellow brick and glass against the deep purple clouded sky. I think I've picked out the window on the second floor, in the room where my brother is not going to die. All the voices behind me say that Duane's not going to die.

Is it being philosophical to believe the voices? I suppose it could be.

Is it being philosophical to be picking up golf-ball-size rocks and whipping them one after another at that window like a spoiled and angry and petulant kid?

Of course it isn't. I'm sorry, Duane. I'm sorry, man. You're not even gone and already I'm letting you down.

HARVEST

"No."

"Eric, what do you mean, no?"

Everyone is speaking in hushed tones, which is what you do. The room is too hot, but it is cold death itself. All bald walls and machines, this room is the opposite of humanity. It's all been so fast, there isn't even a card or a flower anywhere yet.

"I mean no, Ma. Nobody's turning anything off."

"Eric," Dad cuts in, and now I couldn't care less.

"Shut it," I say to him, holding up a *shush* finger, but holding it with my arm fully extended between me and him.

My dad's red-rimmed eyes go altogether wide, but some miracle does in fact shut his mouth. I don't know what I would do if he snapped back at me, or what he would do about what I would do. Everybody's best not finding out, that's for certain.

Ma's face is the exact shade of her pink roses, which she loves more than anything else on God's earth and almost as much as she does God himself. Her cheeks are as wet as if she'd just been sprayed with a spritzer. When she talks, though, she doesn't sound like she's been crying, because that isn't her. Not even now. Moisture appears, without tears, like morning dew.

"We have to decide this together," she says.

"No, we don't," I say. "We haven't been *together* on anything since I was twelve, so we're surely not gonna start here."

"Eric," Dad tries, and this time I don't even give him words. He gets that *shush*-finger warning once more, and I speak to Ma.

"It's too soon for anything like this, Ma. Way too soon."

Her hands are prayer-folded, like they are every morning with her rosary beads. "Son, I know you don't want to hear this—"

"You *know* I don't want to hear it, Mother Superior," I say, to insult her piety as much as to make my point, "and yet, I still hear you talking."

I had already made it clear that I didn't want to hear *this*, when *this* first came up a half hour ago and I stormed out of the room and the hospital and the situation. The doctor had his ideas and his procedures and all that, but I had mine. My solution was to throw rocks. From what I can tell, I've done as much good as he has.

I am seventeen years old. Or I was, before my big shitslice of a brother went diving into the quarry and broke his neck and his skull and my grip on the world. Now I'm about seven.

Full credit to Ma, she's not fazed by me, and she's not blinking from what remains of Duane. Almost wish I had religion now. She makes it look useful.

"He's not getting any better, Eric," she says, almost serenely. "And he's not going to."

I fight an impulse. I fight and I fight and I fight it, and I don't know what it looks like on the outside but inside I am thrashing and punching and clawing at this thing, because while I am not great at impulse fighting, I know this is the right battle.

So, you and Dad aren't getting any better either, but we're letting you live.

That's what the impulse wants to say. But even I know this is wrong. Even now, even I.

I think Duane-ish instead.

"If there is one thing I know in this world, then this is the thing I know," I say, echoing one of my brother's catchiest catchphrases. "Duane belongs to me a hell of a lot more than he belongs to you. This decision is *mine.*"

At seventeen years old I know this decision is not mine. But there's knowing, and there's knowing.

The discussion is over.

"I want some time," I say to them. "We need some time. He told me," I say, pointing beside me to the bandaged and purpled, ventilated hissing husk that is my brother. "We need some time alone. Can we have that?"

Who could say no to that? The only person I know who could say no to that would be the guy on the ventilator, who would do it just for a laugh. Then he'd say, "Just smokin' ya, kids. Take all the time in the world."

All the time in the world.

"Are ya just smokin' us, kid?" I ask when we're alone.

All the time in the world. It's not much.

I climb up next to him into the bed, not looking at the biological version of him but instead the mechanical extensions.

I look at the monitors, listen to the respirator. Then I look at the ceiling. I fold my hands.

I can feel him, though. I can feel his temperature, which is warm, and his heartbeat, which is crazy strong—wildly, encouragingly strong.

Except that's my heart. My heart is beating so hard, I think the nurses might come rushing in to respond to it.

"What am I gonna do?" I ask him, because the pathetic truth is I asked him every important question I ever had.

I should not be surprised when I get no answer. But I'm shocked.

"No, Duane," I say, and I roll over onto my side. There's a tube going into his left nostril and tubes coming in and out of his arms and legs, and I may be doing something wrong but I'm careful and I don't care. His head is all bandaged and his neck all braced, and I snuggle up to him like a baby possum clinging to its mother.

When I was three, I killed my Russian dwarf hamster by love-squeezing it to death. The pediatrician told my parents that was common and normal behavior.

I recognize his mouth. That is my brother's smart mouth. He'd just gotten the mustache the way he wanted it, finally. His Manchu was just Fu enough, he said. I lightly trace the corners of his mouth with my thumb and forefinger.

"I know you better than this," I say. "Come on now, man. I know you better than anybody, and I know you better than this."

I wait, again, for him to do what he's always done best. Defy them all.

I wait.

All the time in the world.

I know this is too much, too much time in here in this place of rules and procedures and time-is-of-the-essence. They're giving me far more time than they should.

"I hate you for this," I say, pinching the corners of his mouth a little harder, a little harder.

I have the hiccups as I shove up off the bed, stomp away out of the room, push past my parents and the ICU nurses and all the rest of them. I have the hiccups.

I'm standing with my back to the river's voices again, arms folded, staring up at the window, when my dad approaches. I feel fury as he gets closer, but I see in my peripheral vision that he's not intimidated the way he should be, and he's not breaking stride. My arms are still folded as he reaches me, puts a firm grip on both my biceps, and says the stupidest thing anyone has ever said.

"It's okay now," he says. "It's okay."

It's been a long time since I wanted to hit somebody with malicious intent. Right now my dad feels to me like a gift from God.

As trade-offs go, God, this is a little weak, but at least it's something.

"If you want to take a shot," Dad says, still right there, staring into my eyes.

That shakes me. It's a shaky day.

"If it makes you feel any better, Son, go right ahead. If anything makes you feel better, go right ahead."

Wow. He doesn't hug me or anything, though. Probably figures if he did, I *would* slug him. Probably right.

We stand there, looking I'm sure every which way of weird to the people strolling by. He holds his grip on my muscles, and I hold my immovable arm-fold, and we stare at each other. A sound eventually comes out of me.

"I have the hiccups," I say.

"I recognize them," he says.

We grip and stare some more. We're both grateful for the river's running commentary.

"We need to go inside, Eric," he says. "We are needed. There is much to do, and some of it is urgent. And while God knows your mother is capable of all of it, he also knows she shouldn't have to be."

I look away from him, and back up to the window, which is only on the second floor but might as well be on a mountaintop.

He gently tugs me where we need to go. I gently allow him to.

"What?" I say when Dad leads me to an office on the floor above Duane's. "What are we doing here when he's down there?"

"Your mother is in here," he says, ushering me in.

Inside I find Ma sitting in a chair with a great fistful of Kleenex like a blue head of cabbage. The main doctor, Dr. Manderson, is sitting next to her in the *comforting* posture I am sure he learned in med school. Wonder if there was a test on it.

"Hello, Eric," says the man whose office it must be, because he comes from behind his teak desk to shake my hand. He greets me with unsmiling warmth as he explains he is David Buick, the unit social worker, and sits me in a chair on the other side of my mother. Dad remains standing by the door. Like the family's strong sentinel, or the one most likely to bolt for the exit.

"Why are we here?" I say, rudely getting to the point.

Just as rudely, though not rudely at all, the point is sent right back to me.

"No," I say expertly now, as "No" is my theme today.

"There is absolutely *no* pressure here," Buick assures me.

"No pressure," Dr. Manderson agrees.

"It is right, Son," Ma says. "It is the right thing . . . the most generous . . ."

"It's what God wants us to do," Dad says.

"What is God's goddamn problem today?" I snap, and pop up out of my chair.

Nobody gasps, or argues with me. Nobody even asks me to calm or sit down. There is no resistance of any kind.

I am left to do it myself.

Pieces of a brother. In somebody else. My brother, my boy. They were his. His heart, his kidneys.

Good God. His *eyes*.

"No. Hell, no. Hell, no," I say, and storm to the door, and back again.

They were his; now they are mine. That is it, and that is right. No more discussion.

"He never signed a donor card, and he didn't have that thing on his driver's license either," I say pathetically, trumping nothing.

My mother allows herself the tiniest of smiles. "He drove for six months without insurance, too."

I feel instantly better, for an instant, as I remember that and how *Duane* that was. Then the hiccups come thundering back.

"Donor card, my ass." That's what Duane would say right now.

Duane would do it, without hesitation. I half suspect he's downstairs right this minute prying out his own pancreas to give to some kid in Ohio in time for the Babe Ruth baseball season.

Of course he would do it.

"No," I say, and no one in the room buys it.

"Time, Son," Ma says. "Time matters."

All the time in the world.

"And Duane is already gone," Dad adds, "while there are a lot of people who—"

"You should know," I say. "You were dead a long time before Duane."

I don't even mean it. There is nothing wrong with the man or with how he is conducting himself right now. I can only imagine what it all feels like for him, and he's carrying it off with dignity I couldn't dream of. He does not deserve this.

"I'll stop talking if you stop talking, Dad."

It's the best I can do. He answers by not answering.

The most silent minute in the most silent room ever— ends with me turning to my mother, the doctor, Buick, and my dad in turn, and nodding once to each.

Like I have any power at all.

There's a two-seater couch along the wall by the door. I walk over to it and lie down. I curl like a boiled shrimp, and sleep while the rest of them get on with the business of harvesting the rest of the best of my brother.

PIECES

Pieces, Duane called them. His little bits o' wisdom, his small philosophies.

"Here's a piece for ya, boyo," he would say when he was getting all wound up and windy. "Self-awareness is a great thing. Unless you're trying to sleep."

CERTIFIED

On the mantel above the fireplace that doesn't work are two things that would make Duane laugh. One is the urn containing his ashes. He would find that impossibly funny without even knowing why. Right next to that is the framed Organ Donor Certificate of Appreciation from the surgeon general. "Thanks for all the guts," he would say, mocking the thing and at the same time loving it. I know he would say exactly that.

It's been a year. I stare at the urn less and less. I look at the certificate less and less. I do the ritualistic ghoulish stuff less and less, and I feel sorry for myself less and less. I think.

But it's been a year. I woke up with that thought on the tip of my brain, and I came right to the urn. I am pretty sure I've been talking to him out loud for several minutes, and this has brought my parents into the room. I see them, their reflection on the yellowed oval mirror behind Duane, and in that reflection we're all together again, the four of us.

"I want to meet them," I say.

Through the people at the organ bank, we have exchanged

letters with some of the recipients of Duane's inadvertent generosity. Some of them choose not to get involved, which is their right whether I agree with it or not. Others sent what sounded like form thank-you letters that could well be mass generated by the people at the organ bank, for all the imagination and personality they convey. Then there were a couple that made me think differently. Made me think "Ouch," but made me think the right kind of "Ouch" and that maybe there was something here that was worth it beyond the goody-goody generality of doing the *right thing*. All of them were anonymous.

If you're looking for more, though, the organ bank will help you.

"I'm looking for more," I say to my folks when they remain frozen in the mirror as if they were a portrait and not a reflection.

"I imagine you are," Ma says. It's an odd sort of interaction we're having through refraction, through dead Duane. But an interaction between us that wasn't odd would be the oddest interaction of all. So we go with it.

"What about you guys?" I ask.

"We've discussed it," Dad says. "We've decided the letters are enough. The letters are a comfort to us."

"We can look at the letters anytime we like," Ma adds, and I notice what a unit they have become. They're closer this past year than I ever remember them being. They weave a conversation together in a way that resembles close harmony singing.

You're laughing at that thought, Duane. I know you are. Great for you, you can laugh. They're right behind *me*.

I can admire it, though, and I do.

"If we meet the people . . . ," Ma says, her voice trailing off.

Dad picks it up. "The people become people. They become relationships. That is more than we can do, Son. We have done what we can do. Now we just want to leave it be."

I see, of course, and I know the rightness of it. I see it in their fading reflections, in their agedness beyond their ages. I don't know what I was thinking before, thinking this was all me and they were on the outside edges. Their relationship with Duane was funny, but not fun-funny. It was rocky and it was rough and it was distant and unfathomable.

And I was a jerk to think any of that mattered in the end.

"I understand, Dad."

"And I understand that you need to do it," he says.

"We both understand," Ma adds. "Just keep in mind this makes the people people."

I nod. "I know that," I say. "That's what I want."

What I don't tell them is that I want something else. I want what they have.

They have this majestic, glorious agony that they reawaken every day just by awakening. They are so much better than me. Every day my Duane pain fades that much more, and they are *right* in their grief. Which is a laugh, because after them doing everything wrong for forever, we have finally staggered into the thing my parents do right, and I want it.

If it is bone-aching sadness, I want it. If it is joy and satisfaction and pride, that would be fine too.

But there is a nothingness that is filling the Duane space in me, spreading like a gradual, internal bleeding. That can't go on.

o o o

Duane's heart is in Bermuda. He would love that. He was an island-lifestyle kind of a guy, and I am sure he would be pleased to know that his heart is beating on in such a place. For some reason the New England Organ Bank, in addition to focusing on the six-state region, also covers the pink sand island. On that island is a man named Mr. Sampson, the sixty-seven-year-old owner of a twenty-one-year-old heart.

How 'bout that. Duane's heart is a year older than Duane ever was. I shake my head thinking about it. Like a lot of thoughts lately, this one shakes me. I should probably expect more of that kind of thing.

But I won't be meeting Mr. Sampson. In response to my very polite letter, Mr. Sampson sent back a better letter expressing the very reasonable fact that he never leaves his island these days. "I walk. If I cannot walk to a place, then I do not go. I take life at a certain pace. And I treat this gift your family gave me as the precious thing it is." However, if ever I am in his neighborhood, he wrote, I am very welcome to stop by.

Of the seven recipients who were the beneficiaries of my brother's healthy-ish life and untimely death, three of them ultimately agree to meet. Another three choose to remain anonymous for whatever reasons of their own. They are certainly not unreasonable to do so, but I do wish I had the opportunity to speak with them, tell them how wrong they are, and perhaps get back the pancreas, corneas, and lung that we so generously gave them.

So, then there were three.

The organ bank coordinates everything, and it is decided that we will gather at the Park Plaza downtown, where we will do the introductions and then sit down to a fancy lunch that will serve as a thank-you to my family—that is, me—a celebration of the ongoing achievements of the donor program, and a chance to swap stories of the various lives involved in this whole swap-shop deal we are in.

Because make no mistake, it's a swap. We know what these guys all got out of it, but I'm still not sure about my end. And I'm looking for something.

It's not lunch exactly.

"Tea?" I say to Ms. Francis, the organ bank's point person for the event. She has a photographer with her, who shoots us shaking hands in the Plaza's lobby. We agreed on this arrangement after Ms. Francis ran through all the possibilities over the phone. Would I be comfortable with unobtrusive local TV coverage? No. Sunday magazine feature? No. Meeting the extended families of the recipients? Well, no. Maybe someday. Maybe everything someday, but this is not that day. Even under normal circumstances I get a little balky meeting groups of unknowns, and on this day especially my tunnel vision is fixed and dilated. They will work up some quotes, promotional stuff, happy visuals for their own website, maybe do a little press release thing, and that will be it.

"Yes, afternoon tea. High tea, you could call it."

I don't like tea all that much. And the restaurant has such a big reputation, I was dreaming about the lunch even while I was eating my breakfast.

"Oh," I say. "Okay. It's just, my stomach might be growling a little bit, that's all."

She reaches out and pats my forearm, which gets

photographed. "Oh, Eric dear, there is food, of course. High tea is much more than just tea."

"Oh," I say. "Cool."

"Right," she says, and leads me toward the restaurant. "Now, two of our guests are here already. We're just waiting on Melinda. But come on in and meet the gentlemen. Are you nervous?"

I was a little nervous before she said that, and I am a lot nervous now. I can't understand it, but I can't control it either.

"No," I say, stupidly.

"Okay," Ms. Francis says with a warm and kind smile that says she knows better. The photographer records this.

"Is he going to be here the whole time?" I ask.

"Once the tea arrives, that's his cue to leave," she says.

"Good."

We walk down the corridor, then through the doors of the swankiest place I have ever been in. It looks like pictures from high school history of where Louis the Sixteenth of France would hang out.

"Wow," I say, staring up and around as I walk, like I was just flown in from a lost civilization rather than seven miles up the road. I hear the click of about ten pictures getting the moment down.

"It's a very nice place," she says. "But no more than we feel our donor families deserve."

By the time I look properly straight ahead, I'm staring across a big circular table at the guys.

To my left one guy fairly leaps out of his seat and extends a hand for shaking. He's so anxious and nervous that he's already doing the vigorous up and down of the handshake before we even make contact. It's like hopping onto a moving trolley, but I catch up and grip his hand. His smile is threatening to jump right off his face, it's so intense, and the feel of his hand is warm and strong. He looks a year or two younger than me, fine-boned and blue-eyed. His skin is near-translucent pale, and his hair is red.

"Phil," he says, introducing himself.

"Eric," I say in return.

It's an extended handshake.

"What are you staring at?" he asks.

"You have red hair," I say awkwardly. I am almost giggling.

"And you have blond hair," he says, still smiling. "Is this important?"

My brother was always great. But he wasn't always good. And he had more special fun at the expense of the ginger-haired population than was strictly humane.

Phil received Duane's inner-ear bones in transplant. I feel like bursting out laughing at the notion of Duane's hearing bones being subjected to awful redhead remarks for the next fifty years.

"It's not important," I say, "but for what it's worth, I think you have great hair."

"Oh," Phil says, withdrawing his hand and running it back and forth over his own head. "Thank you."

Take that, Brother. Now we're having fun.

"Barry," says the other guy, extending a hand. I shake his hand firmly. He shakes firmer. Then firmer.

"Good grip," I say, eventually almost prying my hand out of his.

"I thought you would like to know how healthy I am

today. To be honest, Eric, before I got your brother's liver, I was as weak as a bunny. *You* could have squeezed me into submission."

Well. Okay, then.

"So thanks, is what I mean," he says.

"You're welcome," I say.

"Please, let's sit," Ms. Francis says. "Melinda should be only a few more minutes."

"Over here," Barry says as I'm about to sit next to Phil. He slaps the seat next to him loudly. "We'll take turns."

"It's okay," says Phil.

I walk around the table to the seat next to Barry, who has Phil on the other side of him, then Ms. Francis next to me and the photographer next. The remaining empty seat for Melinda has its back to the entrance.

We are reading the list of treats that actually make up the impressive afternoon tea, and trying to get comfortable with each other. It's hard. The initial hello has its own kind of one-foot-after-the-other easy structure to it, but then it gets clunky. Without the photographer, who snaps *everything*, it might be a little easier. But without Ms. Francis, it would be impossible.

"I have been here for the tea a couple of times before," she says, "and it was truly fabulous."

"That sure is a lot of tea," Phil says.

"I didn't think there were a hundred and fifty different kinds of tea," I say.

"Tea *cocktails*," Barry says, rubbing his hands together. "Now we're talking."

"Oh," Ms. Francis says, "I never noticed those before."

"Well, it would be pretty dull just drinking tea all day," he says.

"How old are you?" I ask him.

"Twenty-one. And can I see a real, non-tea-based cocktail menu too, please?"

"Oh," Ms. Francis says, kind of startled. "People don't usually . . ."

Barry is clearly not swept up in the spirit of the tea-infused operation. I find myself staring at him while he, oblivious to me, stares at the menu. My brother averaged about a beer a week between ages seventeen and nineteen, then stopped drinking completely two years before the law said he could start. He said two beers made him bored and boring and he had better things to do. That liver of his was showroom new.

Whose liver is it, anyway?

"Maybe the tea itself is really good," I say.

Barry looks up at me, grins like we are part of some rascally conspiracy, and claps me on the back of my neck.

"I'm not that interested in *good*," he says. "Y'know? Yeah, you know."

The way he looks at me, into my eyes, with his genuinely amused, smiley eyes, I get the feeling he does believe that I *know*. Y'know?

When I don't answer, he fills the space.

"Funny thing, Eric. Darnedest thing. Before, when I was sick all the time, I had practically no interest in cocktails at all. Take-it-or-leave-it kind of a deal. Then . . . it's like your brother's liver made me thirsty. How funny is that?"

When I stare at him, glare at him for what feels like three hours and his grin does not shift one bit, I give in and answer.

"Insanely funny," I say.

"Nobody can deny God's got a sense of irony, that's for sure. We are gonna be pals, Eric. I can just feel it. Blood brothers, like."

I get a chill, and I don't even know what it means. I don't even know what I think about what he said, so why should I shiver?

"Pals" sounds good. "Blood brothers" sounds good. So?

"What was he like?" Phil blurts out.

When I swing my attention over to him, I find him leaning over the table, into my airspace, with a look like he's bursting. Like he's been aching to get to this and now it just had to jump out on its own without his say-so.

And a whole different feeling comes over me. My stomach swirls, my face gets all flushed. My eyes water, but hold steady. Phil's face looks exactly how I feel, as if just like that he's brought Duane to the table for us.

"Holy moly," Barry says, cutting through the moment and creating a whole different one.

"Melinda," Ms. Francis says brightly, standing up.

All eyes turn to Melinda coming through the door and approaching our table.

I would have to be a far better guy than I am to say that the first thing I notice isn't how pretty Melinda is. She looks like she is in her mid- or late twenties with a lot of thick auburn hair and an altogether that Duane would refer to as überhot. She is beach-volleyball attractive.

Before I can get all the way up to greet her, Barry grabs my arm and says into my ear in a deep rumble-whisper, "I have an organ I'd like to donate to that."

I fall back into my seat. I stare at him, tilting my head like a confused dog, because right now I am as confused as a dog can get. All I can do is stare at him, because I am a million miles from having a response for that. Barry reads something different in my expression, because he is chuckling and nodding like we just collaborated on something great.

"Eric?" Ms. Francis says, snapping me out of it.

I get up now, fumble with my napkin and bumble around the table to greet Melinda. "It's a pleasure to meet you, Melinda," I say, all goofy schoolboy.

She shakes her head at me, opens her mouth to speak, shakes her head some more. She looks very teary as she withdraws her handshake offer and gives me the tightest neck hug I have ever had, without a doubt. "Thank you so much," she says. "You have no idea. This is the most wonderful . . ."

I wonder if photographers reach a point in their lives when they think themselves invisible.

"I think that's enough," I say, waving him away, but not until I am sure he's got this moment in the can. That sad part of me is again thinking that this photo showing up on Boston.com would not be the most awful thing that ever happened. But the better me is hugging her back, feeling proud and right.

"I know you didn't want to meet our family members, not yet anyway," she says, fumbling in her handbag. "But I do hope a photo is okay." She produces the picture before I can say whether it's okay or not.

It is okay. It's of a little boy, about three years old, sitting on the back of a pained- and patient-looking West Highland terrier. Both the boy and the dog have muddy faces. The boy's eyes are laughing, and his mouth is open wide like a manga comic kid.

"I'm gonna guess he's yours," I say, feeling myself do that stupid thing where you half mimic the faces you see in pictures.

"Close your mouth. You're attracting flies," Barry says, bumping up next to me and shaking Melinda's hand.

Phil leans over and likewise joins the greetings. "I didn't know we were allowed pictures," he says. "Eric, you want me to send you some pictures? Everybody wants to meet you, but I could send some pictures."

"Oh," I say, head spinning from the rapid succession of stimuli. "That would be . . . maybe, yeah . . ."

Ms. Francis, being the professional here, gets the situation in hand. "Why don't we all sit down, get to know each other a bit."

While I have not always been the biggest fan of being told what to do, right now it sounds like music. I stare at the picture for several seconds before pocketing it.

Melinda is excited about the selection of teas. She buzzes through the menu, and when the waiter comes by, she orders black tea with ginger and lychee. Melinda knows tea, I think.

Ms. Francis has green tea with oolong and spring blossoms.

I'm afraid when it's the guys' turns, we don't pull it off with the same flair.

"Do you have regular tea?" Phil asks.

The waiter smiles. It's that kind of place, where the staff has way better manners than you do and only laughs at you on the inside. "I'd suggest the Earl Grey," he says, and Phil looks relieved.

"Iced tea?" I ask, and he just nods.

"Do you have pork chops?" Barry asks.

"We actually have a very nice tea-rubbed pork sandwich," the waiter says.

"Oh, yeah. Right," Barry says, looking all around the table. "Tea-rubbed? Is that like a tea joke? He's pulling my pork chop, isn't he?"

"Does he look like a chop-puller to you?" I ask.

Barry regards the man. "Well, yeah. Now that you mention it, he does kinda—"

"He's not joking," Ms. Francis says crisply. Then she addresses the waiter. "That sounds lovely. We will have the traditional tea for five."

"And I'll have a tea cocktail . . . the spiced apple mar-tea-ni," Barry says.

It is already seeming to me like the most surreal tea party of all time. And that includes Alice's.

A piano in the corner tinkles away as we stare around the room and glance fleetingly at each other. There is no player at the piano, as it plays itself. Ms. Francis makes conversation about everybody's commute as the waiter brings all the various parts of the impressive traditional tea. We get scones with cream and jam. Sandwiches—egg salad, chicken salad, salmon, and the famous tea-rubbed pork—cut into triangles and stacked on tiered silver trays. We get a selection of little cakes and chocolate-dipped strawberries and various candied fruits. Lots of tea. Tea keeps coming at us. Barry's mar-tea-ni comes, and goes without my ever seeing him sip it. He orders another. My iced tea is quite good.

"You have to try this," Barry says to me as the second cocktail arrives.

"No, thank you," I say, and the sound of my voice makes me aware of how silent I've been. Ms. Francis is doing all the hard work of trying to turn this into a conversation, but really I'm the engine of this thing and if I don't crank it, then nothing will. There's a brief flare of life when the photographer takes pictures of the lovely presentation of food and we make a decent play of seeming festive with it. Then he's dismissed and things sort of deflate again.

Except, mostly, for Barry.

"When you said this pork sandwich was no joke, it was no joke," he says while chewing on one. "I never knew how magic tea was. Between the pork and the cocktails, I have to say I have sadly underestimated the powers of tea. Is anyone gonna have that last . . ."

Everybody else does that sweeping gesture with their hands to indicate, *No, you have it.* And he does.

Another cocktail arrives.

"I think I will," I say when Barry doesn't offer me a taste again.

"Go for it, go for it," he says.

I go for it.

And it tastes like a glass of Thanksgiving.

"Please," I say, flagging down the waiter and pointing at the glass.

In a few minutes I have my own cocktail. In another minute and a half I have my own half cocktail. Two minutes later I am gesturing to the waiter for another.

I lean across the table, across my beautiful martini glass full of spice and nice, across toward my new redheaded friend.

Friend? Is he that? Is he something more? Something else

entirely? Who are these people? Who are they to me?

"My brother," I say to Phil, "was *mental.*" I say it in a way that I know everybody knows "mental" is the best word there is. Phil smiles big and nods. Then I look around to find that the table has closed in and lightened up. Everybody's listening—even Barry—as everybody has apparently been waiting for pretty much exactly this.

"He was a musician, I believe. Is that right?" prompts Ms. Francis.

"He was," I say. "He was the best. That's him over there right now, playing the piano."

Phil twists to see, and I like him more. Barry slaps my back, and I look over to see Melinda looking at me with an almost motherly soft smile.

"He was a guitar player, Phil," I say, pulling him back to the conversation. "He was a fine athlete, a rascal, a jerk. He had a wicked sense of play, a foul sense of humor, and bad breath, which my mother always said was related to his language. Everybody loved him, except for the people who didn't, but he had an explanation for what *their* problem was, except I can't say it in front of the ladies."

The ladies speak up quickly, definitively, simultaneously on this subject.

"I appreciate that," says Ms. Francis.

"Oh, go on, say it," says Melinda.

That makes everybody laugh.

And now this feels good.

I have a second tea-tini, and already know it will be my last. My limit is usually one. That's beers. My limit on tea-tinis is normally zero.

Barry orders yet another, and something in me rises to this occasion. "And then you're shut off," I say, quite seriously.

He laughs. Then, when I don't laugh with him, he gives me a quizzical arched eyebrow.

"You are cute," he says.

"I don't think I am, no," I say.

"You know what?" he says, putting a heavy arm around me. "We're gonna be great together, kid. This feels right. You need me."

I have nothing for this. I open my mouth, even feel my jaw working, but nothing like words comes out.

"Switch seats," says my new hero, Phil. Showing deceptive strength, he tugs Barry out of his seat and fills it with himself.

"Do you want to tell him anything?" Phil says.

"Huh?" I say.

"Go on," he says. "You've got a direct line. You might as well use it." He leans his ear right up close to my mouth, an inch away.

So, what then, maybe two inches away from the original equipment ear bones of my year-gone brother? The still-living, functioning . . . still *hearing* organic pieces of Duane. I stare at the ear, then imagine I am staring all the way in, like a light in a tunnel, and there he is.

"That was really stupid, Duane," I whisper. "You knew better than that, asshole."

Phil hangs there, leaving me the ear until he's sure I'm done with it. Then he pulls back, looking a bit spooked but another bit satisfied. And very white.

"Anytime, Eric," he says. "You can talk to him absolutely anytime you want, day or night."

And, silly fool that I am, I bite my cheek inside and nod-nod my silent thank-you.

Who are these people? What are they, to me?

The conversation floats, through safe and calm waters, until I notice Melinda checking her watch. The waiter is clearing plates, and Ms. Francis is writing on her palm with an invisible pen to tell him she would like the bill.

"I want to thank you so, so much," Melinda says, pushing back from the table. "This was lovely." She sits there, her hands folded in her lap, biting her top lip with her bottom teeth so she looks childlike and nervous. "I am sorry I didn't have much to say." She takes out an actual pen and notepad and starts writing while speaking. "I hope you didn't mind, Eric. I mostly just wanted to see you, to see . . . Duane's people, or person, or whoever I could touch. I feel so blessed, and I hope you do get at least a little sense of how huge and powerful your family's gesture has been. I have to go . . . I have child care issues . . . but here are all my details, if you ever . . . if there is anything you'd . . ."

I take the paper as she slides it across to me. Then she stands; so I do. We each step around the table, and meet, and it's an embrace.

I know I have never used that word in my life. Probably never even thought it.

Melinda is warm, strong, and soft, and she knows how to hug a person. She squeezes me tight, and I hope this means it's okay to do the same, because I'm doing that whether I like it or not.

And I do.

Then, subtly, she reaches behind her, takes my hand from

behind her back, and slides it down, a bit lower, almost to her waist. Over her kidney.

She leans back to catch my eyes. "Feel it?" she says sweetly. "You feel *him*?"

I nod, look away, feel tremendous relief at the knowledge that the photographer is not here for this.

I do feel him. Right there. Like I haven't in months. Did she know, that that's what I came for? Do people who share . . . whatever it is we share, have a kind of telepathy, a kind of sense of each other? Duane always knew every which way of me inside out. Did that power rest in his kidney?

"I have to go home to my boy now," Melinda says. "You be in touch if you want to. Or don't. If you want to."

She kisses my cheek, holds it for several seconds, and I think my knees should be able to buckle in every direction, they have so many different reasons to.

"Can I have one of those slips of paper?" Barry says as Melinda backs away. She barely glances his way as she gives me a two-hand wave good-bye, and is gone, through the gilded lobby and away.

I am wobbly as I drop into my seat again.

"Good Lord," Barry says. "Be in touch *if you want to*? I would be in touch with every last—"

"Stop it, Barry," I say.

"Tell you what. I'll trade you back the liver for that scrap of paper."

"Grrrr," I say, clenching my fists and pumping half my body's blood up to my head. I whip around to get my face right in his face, and I don't know my own plan but I know it's going to lack loveliness.

"Dude," he says, 100 percent unfazed. "What's happening to your head? Calm down. Think about your blood pressure. I might need your heart some day."

I'm glad that Ms. Francis has gone to question something on the bill, most likely the total of tea-tinis. Because my blood is percolating loudly as I reach maximum boil.

And then, it cools, in an instant. I settle down, lean back, inhale, exhale, and laugh. A little.

"That's just like something Duane would have said," I say, and slap Barry's rotten shoulder.

"I know that," he says, with all the confidence in the world.

Ms. Francis returns, looking slightly shaken by the bill but still composed.

"Well, gentlemen," she says, "I hope this was a worthwhile day for everyone, that we all feel good about what we experienced here today?"

"God, yes," Barry says. "When can we do it again? I can see why people give up organs just to come to one of these things."

"Ah," she says, "well, the organization normally does just organize the one of these. But certainly, if you choose to keep in contact, mutually agreed . . ."

Phil shoves a piece of paper into my hand, then shakes vigorously again, as he does. "Like I said, Eric, anytime. Up to you. Whatever, y'know? It's all there. On the paper. You can always get ahold of me, one way or another. Now I have to run. My mom is picking me up outside. . . . You wanna meet my mom?" he asks with bright-eyed unreasonable hope.

I look at his open, honest ginger-infused self. Poor guy. Duane would have had him for lunch.

"No, Phil," I say, blowing his plane right out of the sky. "But it's nothing personal. Just not now. Maybe sometime."

"Okay," he says, taking that as some kind of high point in the conversation that he doesn't want to jeopardize. He scurries along, far too fast for the Park Plaza lobby, but surely nobody could be offended.

"C'mon, kid," Barry says, an arm draped around me as we head out the front doors of the Plaza. "I'm gonna show you what a *real* high tea is all about."

Two emotions sweep over me. The first is fear, stupidly enough. Something about Barry actually has me back on my heels and intimidated as if he has some control over me, which he surely doesn't have.

The second, of course, is my old friend anger. And as usual, my old friend rules the day.

"Listen to me," I say, grabbing him by the shirt and growling into his nose. His supreme confidence suffers a fracture, and I see it in his expression. I've seen it before, and know it when I strike it. "You got a big piece of something that belongs to me in there," I say, using my free hand to poke him in the solar plexus. "You need to treat it better than you're treating it today. Or else."

He puffs a breath of apple and vodka into my face.

"Doesn't belong to you," he says. "Maybe it's you who belong to me instead."

"Eric," Ms. Francis calls from a few yards up the pavement. She appears to know something is up without knowing more than that. "Let me drop you off. My car is just this way."

I look at her, wave, then look back at Barry. I let him go,

and offer my hand for a good squeeze, which he does not accept and lets hang for a few seconds.

"It was good to meet you, Barry," I say.

"Or else *what?*" he says.

"Take care," I say, walking away. "Take good care."

"See you around," he calls.

"Or not," I call.

We drive along in silence for fifteen minutes before Ms. Francis says, "I think that was good."

"It was," I say. "It was good. Thank you for that. Thank you for everything. I wish my parents would have gone. They would have loved the high tea."

"Each to his own way," she says, as I am sure she has said countless other times, to countless other un-whole families. "The important thing is to know that the thanks, the appreciation, is all to you folks."

That seems to be the place to leave it. I don't feel like I want to be thanked anymore.

She maneuvers the car the last few blocks, few turns, onto my street, and pulls in front of the house. I get one last handshake—another thing I can do without for a while now—and I get out of the car. Before going I lean in, because I just have to ask.

"Who are these people? Who are they, to me? Who am I, to them?"

She looks up to me from the low driver's seat, offering me no words and a smile that is both angelic and apologetic.

PIECES

"Everything monumental happens to you in summer. Or unhappens."

HORIZON

I wake up at least once in the middle of every night, which never used to happen. And when I wake, I still have a brother, for one or two or three minutes. Then it comes back to me.

When he left, my roster of close friends diminished by around 100 percent, give or take.

Something else got submarined. That was the summer I was planning to go into the military. I had graduated high school, visited the recruiting offices, and was making up my mind. Probably it was going to be the navy. Probably definitely. I have a thing for the ocean, the haunted space of it, the hugeness and all that unknown depth of it. Really, there was always just the one front-runner, the navy, but I still felt I needed to look into the others because of the navy's one primary drawback.

Every time I thought about being canned in on a ship, with fifteen hundred other jerks and nowhere practical to escape to without likely drowning, I had to pause.

But I can be a team player. I had been on a lot of teams

in my stupid sports days, without necessarily loving the teammates.

Anyway, the *event* happened and paused everything. I was incapable of making any real decisions. Or any unreal ones. So that was that for then.

Even though that should have been a different that. Because at least with Duane gone it eliminated the biggest jerk of them all who ridiculed me and rode me with such vigor that I had to conclude he was doing it not for his own amusement—which was why he did *everything*—but because he maybe really didn't want me to go.

Well, too bad, sucker. You went first, so I might as well go now.

It's a year later, twelve long sorry months of getting more sour and less useful to anyone other than a military operation, and so the writing appears on the big wall for me. I paused long enough for respect and confusion. This summer is it for me, and this town and this life, and I predict that once I see that high seas horizon, I won't be back here in any meaningful way again.

My parents think it's a good idea, as they thought it was a good idea last year.

I'm going anyway.

The notion of coming and going from ports all over the world, of staying away from land for weeks or months at a time while spending long hours staring out over the edge of the world over the side of a ship, all that suits me right down to my toes. I have always been this way, more or less, for whatever reason. I get along okay with people, for a time. I like meeting people and then unmeeting them again. The one poet we studied in school who ever made any sense to me was a woman from Maine. Can't remember her name but she said both of the two smartest things I have ever heard from a poet: "There isn't a train I wouldn't take, no matter where it's going," and, "I love humanity; it's just people I can't stand." Or something like that.

Okay, I am mostly talking about taking boats no matter where they're going, but, same idea. I just want to go.

I am in my room, going over the recruitment literature for the fiftieth time, when my dad calls up to me. This never happens anymore. Why would it?

So it is with suspicion that I leave my room and head to the top of the stairs. It's a curving staircase, with a landing halfway up. The rust-colored carpet is worn naked on the edge of each step.

"What?" I ask, looking at the landing, since I can't see around corners.

"Company," he says.

This is either a joke or a level-three shocker. And he doesn't joke.

I come down the six steps to the landing, and look down to the foyer.

"God," I say. "Oh . . . God."

It's Little Martha, Duane's oldest, truest love aside from me. She's not really that little, almost as tall as me, but he got the nickname from a song and hung it on her like a pearl necklace. She left him, about six months before he died, to go out in the world, help the world, make it a slightly better place.

"Stay here and make *me* a slightly better place," he said.

I remember that clearly. She hurt him, and I watched. They were funny like that, never minding playing out life in front of me.

Stay here and make me *a slightly better place*, was what I thought at the time. I loved her every bit as much as Duane did, and Duane knew it, and that was okay. Fortunately, I was harmless. Unfortunately, I was harmless.

She's been off for a year and a half now, helping Africa or eastern Europe or someplace feel better about themselves.

"Hi," I say, with a stupid little wave.

"Hi," she says, mimicking me. "I didn't know."

"Now you know," Dad says, and makes his way away.

Without any discussion about it we both know where we are headed. I always had a thing for the cemetery, always, long before I knew anybody there personally.

But it's not even his cemetery, strictly speaking. His organs are scattered like scarecrow's straw, and the cinders of the rest are, funny enough, in our living room.

But there is a stone, a memorial under a dogwood in the sprawling death-garden of the crematorium. And the name on it is Duane.

"How was Africa, Little Martha?" I ask, draped as cool as ivy over a branch above the stone marker.

She is sitting cross-legged, over the part where my brother's body would be buried. She has her hands extended, toward the stone, like begging.

"You probably shouldn't call me that now. Nobody does."

Another thing he took with him.

"Sorry," I say. "Martha."

"And it wasn't Africa; it was Central America. Guatemala, Honduras. It was good. It was just what it was supposed to be. I'm glad I went. It was time to come home. . . ."

They didn't communicate with each other, that was the deal. She was going to come back when the time was right, or she wasn't. If she did, she'd surprise him.

I'd say they surprised each other.

She hops to her feet, brushes off. "I don't want to be here," she says.

I step down, still being cool. I salute my brother, tell him "Adios, dude," because that is the kind of slinkster cool cat I am.

"Cut the crap, hard-man," she says, cutting my fake legs right off and taking me by the hand.

I have not walked hand in hand with anyone since my mother was dragging me to the dentist at about age seven. This feels a lot better and a little worse.

"Did you talk to my dad?" I ask after a minute.

"Does anybody really ever talk to your dad?"

"I suppose not. What about Ma?"

"What about her? I heard her in the other room, but she never came out."

Martha is still in the first stages of pulling this together. She was, when I knew her before, about the togetherest person anywhere. Right now she strides like an Olympic speed-walker, dragging me to keep up. Every few seconds her hand flies up and covers her mouth and she shakes her head.

"Do you want to hear stuff?" I ask.

She removes her hand. "Of course I want to hear stuff." Her hand goes back up.

"Where are we going?" I ask.

"Stuff," she snaps.

"He was on life support. We had to shut it off."

Her breathing gets quicker and shallower, though I know she is triathlon-fit. It's like she's whistling through her fingers. She squeezes my hand really hard.

"I told them they couldn't," I add.

"Good for you," she breathes.

"But then we did it."

She nods.

"Then they asked . . ."

"Organ donation," she says for me.

"Yeah," I say, and suddenly I find my breathing catching up to hers. "And I said no to that, too."

She's nodding, breathing, and speaking for us both now. "But you did it."

"Yup."

The two of us stop talking now, and slow down to a more pedestrian pace.

"My hand is getting kind of sweaty," I say.

She doesn't answer, she doesn't release.

I tug on her hand, slow her further, tug harder and pull her to stop and face me.

"Somebody has Duane's eyes? Eric?" She is shaking her head no, no, no, tears flying off her face like a sprinkler.

I bump her forehead with mine to stop her.

"He only had eyes for you," I say.

She stares at me all dead-eye fish. Then growls, "That is exactly something your stupid-ass brother would say."

"Thank you," I say.

"Thank you," she says.

o o o

We wind up at the town's ancient pharmacy with the fountain unchanged from the 1930s. Old Geoff, who has been running the place since my parents were doing whatever it was they did in the lead-up to marriage, goes a little wideeyed weird at the sight of me and Martha hopping up onto the creaking chrome stools.

"Martha," he says, like a sweet silly old geezer.

"Hiya, Geoff."

His thick, thick glasses are fogging with nostalgia. "The usual?"

"Of course."

"Same for you, Duane?" he says, turning away toward the fountains.

Martha puts a hand on my hand and shakes her head for me to let that pass.

The lime rickeys are made with syrup that's almost certainly been sitting there since the real Duane had his last one. There's nobody else in here. There is usually nobody else in here.

"You know I have to meet them, Eric."

"Ummm, you mean all of them?"

"All of them you've connected with."

I run over the short roster in my head.

"Ummm, all of them?"

"Yes, all of them."

"How 'bout two of them, and we'll call it a deal?"

She puts her hands on her hips in such a way that it makes her fingers look unfeasibly long and her waist look impossibly slim. Duane always commented on the thrill of the *older woman* aspect of her, though she only had him by two years.

She's got me by five.

"What are you doing with your face?" she says.

"Sorry. Nothing. Anyway, it's kind of complicated, the donor-recipient-family thing—"

"I am family," she says with such authority that she may now outrank my mother on the masthead.

And enough authority to remind me she is, of course, family, and I will need to remember that. She is as much a piece of Duane as his liver is.

Jeez, his liver.

"If I know one thing in this world . . . ," I begin.

"Then this is the thing I know," she finishes, voice cracking at the memory.

"That Miss Martha gets what Miss Martha wants," I say.

Her hand is back at her mouth and she's talking through it.

"Well, for once he was wrong about something, huh?" she whispers. "The bastard."

I raise my glass, "The bastard."

She spins on her counter stool. It squeals. She does a complete turn, taking in the whole tired old place, and it is indeed ghostly. Then we are dew-eyes together.

"He's not *here*, Eric," she says incredulously.

I have been in this zone already. A lot.

I do a full squeaky spin.

I shrug.

PIECES

Watching the news on TV. Duane had just returned from one of his beloved music festivals, unscathed. He frequently returned scathed, in one form or another. Arrested, fined, warned for overexcitement resulting in stage invasion, perhaps. Lost his tent, one time. Lost his wallet more than one time. Broken nose resulting from friendly fire. A new ear-piercing that was, in fact, a full number two pencil. These were mostly his descriptions, so there was always room for interpretation as to what actually transpired.

He looked tired this time, but smiley and serene and so . . . great. The news was showing highlights. We were slumped together watching festival high jinks, including one guy at the top of a human pyramid waving a Canadian flag while wearing a too-small Philadelphia Flyers jersey and nothing else. Duane was philosophical about it.

"There, but for the grace of God, go I," he said sagely.

I got off the couch and went up close to the TV.

"Duane, that *is* you."

"Is it?" he said, sitting up straight now. "Well done, me!"

HOME COOKING

"I suppose maybe we could go to tea with them or something."

There is a sustained silence on the other end.

"Tea? Eric, did you just suggest going to tea?"

"I did, yes. They have the most wonderful high tea at—"

"My goodness. How long have I been away, *Iceman*?"

It has been a long time since anybody called me that. I was a bit rough around the edges when I was kid-like. Feels like it makes as much sense now as *Little* Martha.

I laugh, thinking about the difference, and how the tea thing must sound. "Well, that's what we did before, when we all got together. It was paid for by the donor bank people, though, and they only do it once, and I think it's out of our price range."

She gives me some more phone silence.

"I wish you wouldn't do that," I say.

"Are you still weird, Eric?"

I sigh. "Fine, go back to the silence."

"I mean, like when you used to worship death and play with lizards and try to kill people with sticks?"

This is a gross mischaracterization, and she knows it. And, anyway, I stopped all that stuff before she even went away.

"You know I'm not *still weird*, Martha."

"Fair enough. Let me rephrase. Are you weird *again*? I mean, without Duane? Duane was in a lot of ways your only—"

"I'm fine."

"Okay. Maybe I'm just projecting, because I'm not so fine. I keep looking for him, Eric. I mean, physically as well as emotionally. Like I expected him to be here when I got back, and I'm still expecting him to turn up. I mean . . . he is *going* to. I feel it that strongly."

This is the best news I have heard all year.

"The boy was a force, wasn't he?" I say.

"*Is*. He *is* a force."

"True enough. Now, in the meantime while we await the second coming, you still want to get together with his other parts before he pulls himself together?"

"Yes. Right now."

"Not sure how *now* we can make it, but I'll get to work. You want to meet them at maybe a cheap restaurant or coffee shop or something?"

"Here."

"Huh? There?"

"Here."

"Why there?"

"I don't know. I just thought of it. Feels right. Feels comfortable, and I think I will need to feel comfortable. And I'm already here, so we are already partway there."

Hmmm.

"And you wanted to know if *I* was weird."

"I didn't say I wasn't, Eric. C'mon now. Go arrange this.

Tell them I will cook. Maybe a barbecue or something. It'll
be tremendous. Go, go."

"Okay, I'm going. I only have the direct contact details of
two of them so . . . are you *sure* two won't be enough?"

"Eric."

"Right. I'll contact the donor bank about the last one."

I get off the phone with Martha, and I stare at it before
dialing again. Then, with some effort, I get in gear and get
through to Ms. Francis. I tell her what I need.

"Are you sure, Eric?" she says, something like alarm in her
voice.

"Yes, Ms. Francis. It's kind of important."

"I'd say it must be, if you want to engage with that . . .
personality again."

"Personality. He sure was that, wasn't he?"

"Yes. . . . Well. I will have to contact him myself"—she
sighs unapologetically at the prospect—"to ask if he is interested, since he didn't give you his details in person."

"Okay," I say, and leave her to it.

I proceed to what figures to be the simpler assignment.

"Phil?" I say when he picks up on one ring.

"Yes. Eric? Is this you, Eric?"

"Wow," I say. "Pretty good, considering we only met that
one afternoon."

"Well, I have to confess I've kind of guessed it was you a
few times already this week. I was wrong the other times."

The kid is already not like anybody else I have known.
The fact that his sweetness makes me suspicious does not
speak well to my character, I suppose.

"You're a trip, Phil."

"Good. That's good, right?"

"I'm almost sure it is. Listen, I have a thing to ask you."

"Sure. Sure. Sure."

"I'd like to get together again."

"Yes. Yes."

"Right. Shush for a second while I fill you in. It's not for me so much."

"Oh," he says dejectedly.

"Really, shush now, Phil. It gets better. Somebody else wants to meet you. Somebody really special. Her name is Martha. She was Duane's girlfriend . . . No, that's a stupid word. She wasn't his girlfriend. She was something different, something different and way more than that. But anyway, she was away until recently and she's piecing together the pieces, like I was, and so now she seriously needs to—"

"Now? I could come over now. I know you told me to shush, but I got the point and you were kind of rambling a little, and I am free right now . . ."

Funnily enough.

"No, not right this minute. I'm just making first contacts, trying to organize a little something, to make sure that all you guys are willing and available at the same time in the next week or so."

There is a hesitation.

"All us guys? You mean the terrible guy is going to be there too."

At least it doesn't appear I rushed to judgment on that one.

"Ah, Barry's not so terrible. High spirited, maybe. Edgy."

"And terrible. But that's okay, whatever. I am a yes. And really pretty much anytime will work for me. Just let me know. Thanks for this, Eric. Thanks, really. It's a nice, nice idea. Who knows, maybe even . . ."

My attention to Phil's actual words drifts off on a thought of my own that rolls in. Then I cut him off, gently.

"Hey, Phil?"

"Yeah?"

"Which ear are you listening to me with, right now?"

"Oh," he says warmly. "Uh, it's the *other* one. You want me to switch?"

"D'ya mind?"

"Don't be crazy. Of course not. Here you go. And I won't listen in, I promise."

"You're a pal," I say, and I hear him fumble-switch.

"Hey, man," I say to Duane's bones. "Martha's home. She came back for you. We won't let her get away again, huh?"

I don't know if I'm expecting Duane to respond, to tell me "Good job" or what, but I hang there on the words for a few extra seconds. I feel a little dumb, since obviously it's just his hearing bones and not his speaking bones in there.

"Uh . . . Eric?"

"Hey, Phil," I say, vaguely surprised.

"I didn't hear anything, I swear."

"You're a good man."

I hang up, prepared to continue down my call list, when the phone rings first. It's Ms. Francis.

"Well, I spoke with Barry. Unfortunately, or fortunately, he says he is reluctant to give you his contact details."

"What? What's his problem?"

"He says how does he know you're not going to start stalking him or something. He claims you acted peculiarly at the

Park Plaza, and he isn't confident you are the type of character he should get mixed up with."

Martha gets what Martha wants. Martha gets what Martha wants.

"Um, Ms. Francis, is it acceptable for me to say how outrageous that sounds to me, coming from that character?"

"It is acceptable. Especially since he sounded like he was enjoying saying these things. If I were you, Eric, I would look at this as a blessing in very little disguise. I did pass your details on to him, in case he chooses to be in touch with you at some point."

"Okay, Ms. Francis. Thank you for all your help. It almost certainly is for the best. Thank you."

"Good luck with everything, Eric."

She hangs up, I hang up, my phone rings.

"So, now look who's begging for an audience with the prince."

He sounds slightly more wicked over the phone.

"Nobody's begging for anything, Barry. It's just I thought maybe you would like to get together again for—"

"Why, so you can judge me some more? Just because your brother is dead, is that supposed to mean I have no feelings?"

My, oh my, is this gonna be heavy lifting.

"I never judged—"

"You hurt my feelings."

That would seem to be an impossibility. Mentioning that would probably not help with getting Martha to meet Barry. And I have come to believe that I need Martha to meet Barry, so we can be done with him for good.

"I'm sorry if—"

"I wanted to hang out with you."

"Could you stop cutting off my—"

"You accused me of not taking care of Duane's liver."

I hate the way he says that name. Like they were pals.

"I don't think I—"

"And I happen to really appreciate the liver, thank you very much. It feels great. It's a quality liver. Fits me like a dream. I suspect me and Duane were very similar people, like we have a connection, a deep and mystica—"

I hang up. If Martha's gonna get what Martha wants, she's gonna have to want something other than that nut job.

"Melinda?" I say, having dialed quickly to avoid any possible Barry callbacks.

"No!" the high voice says with some enthusiasm.

"Oh," I say, checking the slip of paper again. "Oh, do I have the wrong number? Sorry. Is Melinda there?"

"No!" is the response again, followed by giggling, followed by crackling, followed by growling.

"Give me that, you," comes a different voice, and it's Melinda's. There is more growling, crackling, giggling, before, "Hello?"

"Melinda? Hello. This is Eric."

"Oh, Eric, hello. Listen, sorry about that. My little boy picked up the phone. Then he gave it to the dog."

"So now I guess I've met the whole family . . . have I?"

As soon as I've said it, I realize I've been a bit forward. What business is it of mine if there is a man of the house? And what do I care? Just asking, is all.

"That's it," she says, more friendly than she might have. "That's the happy household, just Dean and Skye and me."

"Those would be the two rascals from the picture, yeah?"

"The very two."

Well, this is going quite nicely. I've almost forgotten why I called.

"Are you calling for anything in particular?" she says. "Not that you have to be. Like I told you at tea, anytime, for any reason."

"Thank you, that's nice. But, yeah, actually, I do have something. My brother's girlfriend—well, not exactly. Oh, forget that—Martha's her name. And she's been away, working with the peace corps or somebody down in Central America, and, well, she is really close to the family—special, like. And she didn't know, about Duane. Until just about now. And . . ."

"She wants to meet?"

"Yeah, that's it. Wow, I guess I told that better than I thought."

"No, not really," she says, laughing warmly.

"Oh."

"But of course. I mean, obviously I have to work around scheduling issues here, but with a little notice I can usually work out something with a babysitter."

I have the picture out now, of the little guy happily squashing the agreeable mutt.

"Maybe you could just bring Dean?" I suggest.

"Oh," she says. "Oh. Maybe. You think that would be all right? I mean, that might be kind of nice."

"Absolutely," I say. "Hey, bring Skye, too. This'll be a ball."

I am quite excited about the whole idea now, and phone Martha right away.

"So let me see if I have this straight," she says. "You didn't manage to bring one of the three recipients of Duane's pieces, but you did invite somebody's dog."

"You don't have to make me sound quite so lame."

"I'm just kidding. This is getting very exciting. I mean, now a little boy, too. What did you say his name was?"

I am staring at his picture.

"Dean. I think he's, like, three."

"Dean. I love it. So, what do you think, what does this make you, kind of Dean's uncle? Uncle Eric?"

God. God, what is all this? Why do I keep getting blind-sided by new things, new angles, new possibilities?

Who *are* these people?

PIECES

"It's a long fall, off a high horse. Remember that, Brother."

WHEN IN ROME

"Let me see it again," Martha says.

I've never seen her like this. You'd think she was interviewing for the job of her life, or getting married or something. Her substantial cool has blown right out the window, and she flutters around taking care of all the little details she took care of already. Potato salad, three-bean salad, corn bread all sit waiting on the table. Meat is marinating. Drinks are chilling. Because of the insane rain, there will be no outdoor grilling, but that just makes it all the simpler, I say.

She has looked at the photo a dozen times today.

"Here," I say waving it in front of her eyes. "See, he's already that much older than the last time you looked."

"Oh, he is just darling," Martha says. Like she said the other times.

I laugh, but pat her shoulder like a minder as well. "Be cool, Martha. You're gonna freak them out."

"No, I won't," she says, and even when she is flustered, she is more together than me. "I'm excited because this is like a kind of magic, like a sorcerer of some kind bringing back Duane just that little bit in different forms, in different places."

"Like when Mickey Mouse chopped up the big broom into all those spooky little brooms in *Fantasia*," I say, to be a wise guy.

"Yes," she yelps, "exactly that."

Well, I tried, anyway. There will be no derailing Martha's mad optimism today.

My phone rings. It's Phil.

"Hey," I say, "what's up?"

"I can't seem to find the address. I think I am on the right street, but I don't see the house."

"It's Phil," I tell Martha. "He's outside."

Martha's place is a nicely proportioned one-bedroom apartment on the second floor of a building that used to be some kind of factory. There is, on the street side, something she calls a balcony but that in reality isn't up to holding more than a couple of plant pots. It does have a nice sliding glass door, though.

I go there and slide the door open. To see Phil. Sitting on a 50 cc motor scooter at the curb on the opposite side of the street, staring at the whole wrong set of buildings. Also, there is another person on the back.

"Turn around, Phil," I say into the phone.

He turns, sees me waving, then returns the wave with gusto.

"He has company," I say.

Martha comes right over. "What?"

"I guess he thought he was allowed a date," I say, shrugging.

"It's kind of the way with summer barbecues, right?"

"It's not a barbecue. It's pouring outside."

It certainly is. Phil and the mystery date are getting pounded by the rain. She is sitting patiently while he places his helmet on the sidewalk and then takes a big cylinder sort of a thing from her. Then she swings down off the scooter.

"He's a *redhead?*" she squeals.

"Yup."

"How perfect is that?" she says. "I mean, I love him already. I can't wait to talk to those ear bones."

I run down the stairs and greet them at the door.

"Hello. So glad you could make it."

"Thanks for having us. Eric, this is my mom, Dolores. Mom, this is the famous Eric."

Dolores's jacket is not waterproof. And it isn't soup proof, going by the large carroty stain around her stomach and thighs.

"Thank you so much," she says, shaking my hand.

I practically haul her into the building out of the rain. They are clearly the polite types who would have stood there getting pelted as long as I was going to be oaf enough to let them. Phil follows her, one helmet dangling off of each arm, and the dripping Tupperware of soup in his hands.

When we get up the stairs and inside the apartment, Martha is a visible mash-up of conflicting impulses.

"Oh," she says, rushing right up to Phil and hugging him mightily. Her voice cracks on the third repetition of "hello," then she steps back to look at him and bursts out laughing. "Your hair, it's amazing. And ironic."

"I've heard lots of stuff about my hair," Phil says, "but that's the first time for 'ironic.'"

"Martha," I say, gesturing to our female guest, "Phil's mom, Dolores."

"Dolores, so sweet of you to come. Oh, my goodness, the two of you are sponges. Let me get you something—"

"No, no," Dolores says, waving her away.

"Yes, yes," Martha insists. "You have to at least let me get you a couple of sweatshirts while your other stuff dries."

The guests relent, and in a few minutes they are looking relatively cozy in a couple of sweatshirts from Martha's thrift-shop collection of university sweats. Dolores is in a forest-green Dartmouth number, while lucky Phil goes for yet more red, from Boston University.

"Now, that's more like it," Martha says as she starts throwing strips of steak into a big wok. The rest of us are sitting at the drop-leaf table with all the platters set out. I am eating the carrot and coriander soup.

"This is amazing," I say to Dolores, who nods shyly.

"You know," says Martha, "Duane and I talked about getting one of those scooters just like yours. I so wish we did. Do you love it?"

"We do," Phil says.

It is becoming apparent that Dolores is a woman of few words.

My phone bings. It's a text. From Barry. "You never call me," it reads.

I sigh.

"Please, help yourselves," I say to the guests.

"Absolutely," Martha says. "I'll have this done in a couple of minutes."

They go for the hospitality, and my phone rings.

It's not a text, and it is thankfully not Barry. It's Melinda.

"Hi," I say, figuring it's another call for directions.

"Hi, Eric. I am so, so, so sorry, but we aren't going to be able to make it. We were all set to come, but Dean has just been sick all over the place. It's probably nothing serious, but I can't chance it, and I don't think it would be fair to your other guests either. I just feel awful—"

"No, no, of course not. Don't be silly. You have to do whatever is right for Dean."

Martha comes rushing over. "What?" she says.

"Dean's sick, so they can't make it."

"Who's Dean?" Phil asks.

"Melinda's little boy," I say.

"Who's Melinda?" Dolores asks.

"I told you, Mom. She's another one of us, who got things from Duane."

Martha gestures for me to give her the phone. When I hesitate three nanoseconds, she takes it by force. "Hi, Melinda," she says gently, walking toward the wok.

"What did Melinda get?" Dolores asks.

"Mom, come on. We're eating."

"A kidney," I say, though I'm putting more effort into trying to hear the other conversation than this one.

"That's nice," Dolores says, then gestures at the potato salad.

I watch them, Phil and his mom, and see that, well, they certainly don't resemble the family units I'm familiar with. They sure don't resemble mine. But there is something in the way they talk to each other, gesture, respond. She pats his hand lightly as he places the salad bowl by her hand. She points at the BU lettering across his chest, without commenting, and with just the hint of a smile.

I wonder if it took an extra long time to realize his original hearing bones were corroded, because of the infrequency of speech in their household.

"Yes, yes, yes, yes, yes," Martha says with some enthusiasm. "That would be terrific. Okay, you do that. Go take care of that boy, and we will see you then. Bye."

She comes skipping over to the table, flipping my phone to me and bouncing it off my chest. It appears that the near disaster has turned into something else.

"Guess where we're going next Saturday?" she says, poking the tip of my nose with her index finger.

"Disney World?"

"Nope. We have been invited to little Dean's fourth birthday party."

"You're kidding me?" I say.

"I am not."

She stands there bouncing on the balls of her feet in a way that says not only is she not kidding, but it could well be her own birthday party she's discussing. Sizzle and smoke catches her attention back at the stove, and she happily runs after it.

A minute later she is plunked down with the rest of us, and passing around a steaming platter of heavenly-smelling teriyaki rump steak strips.

"Oh," Phil says, with a sheepish wince and a shrug as he takes the platter. "These are awesome. But Mom's a vegetarian."

"Philip," she says, almost snaps, but doesn't. "Stop that. I am not."

Martha laughs, points at her. "Oh, Dolores, please. We are all family, right? No airs and graces here. Tofu pups or spicy bean burger?"

She looks down at her plate, then up again. "Bean burger?"

"Now we're talking," she says, and dashes back to the stove.

While Martha does that, we continue on the wonderful soup and all the other dishes, and I pass around the photo.

"Isn't he great?" I say, and for the first time, maybe, I hear it.

The pride in my voice. Over this little boy. Who I've never even met.

"And who is he?"

"Is Uncle Eric showing off again?" Martha says, delivering Dolores's burger, then sitting beside me.

"Oh, he is a handsome little boy, though," Dolores says.

"He's great," Phil says. "The dog's a little scary. I was bitten by one of them before."

"They all bite him," Dolores says with a giggle just before she bites into her burger.

"It's true," he says, "they do. This steak is incredible, it really is."

"Have all you want," Martha says. "We were expecting more guests."

My phone bings again. Barry again. "You cannot keep me out forever," he texts.

Sheesh. I have to respond. "I was not keeping you out, dipstick. I was trying to invite you in."

"That is so rude, in the middle of dinner. With guests," Martha says.

"Sorry," I say. "You're right, I'm sorry."

"Oh," Dolores says. "But we are family, like you said, right?"

"Still," Martha says. "Manners. Even among family."

Bing.

She stares at me. I start to slowly lower my gaze.

She snags the phone out of my hand, starts reading the text.

Her mouth falls open. "Oh, jeez . . . and I thought *you* were rude. This is disgusting."

"That would be Barry," I say.

"The terrible guy who has Duane's liver?" Phil asks.

"Well, he's not exactly terrible," I say, halfheartedly. Quarter-heartedly.

Martha starts texting.

"What are you doing?" I say.

"I am telling him who I am and that I would like to meet him."

"Oh, Martha, really?"

She nods, types, sends.

The phone rings twenty seconds later.

"Well, hello to you, too, Barry," she says, giving me a triumphant nod that I am certain is premature. She did great on the phone with Melinda, sure, but this ain't no Melinda.

Then we all go quiet, listening while Martha listens. When her eyebrows arch high, I know we're heading into Barrytown.

"I don't see what difference it makes what I am wearing right now, Barry," she says, then listens a bit more. "I don't think I will text you a photograph, no."

Suddenly she thrusts the phone at me. "He wants to talk to you."

"Yeah, hi, Barry, hi. Well, she's wearing cutoff jeans, really short—"

Martha punches me really hard on the arm, and I laugh. The guests may be a little traumatized. I can't quite tell.

"I hung up on him as soon as you handed me the phone," I say rubbing my arm vigorously.

"Good," she says. "But just so you know, I still want to meet him."

"Grrr," I say at her.

"Grrr all you want," she says.

"I hope you don't mind if I say so," Dolores says, "but you make a very lovely couple."

Yikes.

Martha makes a friendly loud cackle noise and reaches over to shove me sideways. Which pretty much settles that couple issue.

The from-scratch caramel-apple pie with custard that Martha presents after the meal is something that countries go to war over. She serves it with an herbal tea that is so good, I can actually taste it. Ginger-lime. All four of us are sitting back in that over-satisfied, belly-patting posture, when the subject of the scooter comes back up.

"I might still get one," Martha says, pushing from the table and going to the window to have another look. The rain has let up some, but still comes down steadily enough to give the conversation a backing track. "It is one of the clearest visions I have of me and Duane, the two of us tooling around town, going to the beach, being all pavement-café-jerkwady about the whole thing. We would have been so unbearable, it would have been fabulous."

Nobody adds anything as she stares out and sips her tea.

"It's a regret," she says into the mug.

Phil is moved by this. There is a little bit of Popeye's *This is all I can stand, I can't stands no more* to the way he firmly puts down his fork and cup and gets up. He goes to the front door and picks up the helmets from the floor where he left them, then marches over to the lady of the house.

At first she doesn't notice him, lost as she now is with Duane in the rain.

Like a dog wanting to be walked, he silently nudges her, with the helmet.

"Would you like to go for a ride, Martha?" he says as if he invented politeness himself.

She turns to him, and the fracture of her features is there for us to see now. Then, as she looks at his earnest, intense gallant little self, the fractures pull themselves together and she beams at him.

"Of course I would like that, Phil. That is a fantastic idea." She scuttles over to the table, where she slaps her mug down, then turns back to Phil. She seizes him by the shoulders and leans close to his right ear. "Eat your heart out, Duane. I'm going scooting with the redhead."

Phil smiles, a little embarrassed as she pulls back. He points, at his left ear. "He's in here," he says.

"Whoops," she says, grabs him again, and says it all again.

"Don't mind us," Dolores says as they head out the door. "We'll just be here getting to know each other better."

I hadn't thought about this end of the equation. Kindness and strangers have never been a big part of my game before. She is a sweet woman, but I still hope it's a short spin on the bike.

We make our way to the window to watch the departure.

"The rain has stopped," Dolores says. "Would you like to step out onto the balcony?"

I look down at the balcony-lite and its four five-gallon pots of plants. "Don't see how that's really possible, unless we displace the plants—which I don't really want to do. How 'bout we slide open the door, though?"

"Lovely," she says, and I slide the glass over.

There is, actually, still a bit of a mist thing happening, though it's not at all unpleasant.

"Look, the sun is peeking out," she says.

I look, but don't see it. "Yeah, looks like, could happen."

Martha is on the back of the scooter seat, helmeted and ready to go. She looks pulse-racingly adorable. Phil, fumbling around, drops his helmet onto the ground with a *thwank*. Twice.

"Don't you worry about her," Dolores says, squeezing my shoulder. "My son is a very safe driver."

"Oh," I say, "I'm sure he is. I'm not worried. And we're not a couple, by the way."

It only sounds that bad after I say it. Like it would be okay for them to crash since she is not my girlfriend. That would not be okay.

As they pull away from the curb, Martha, one hand around Phil's waist, waves up to us madly. My heart accelerates with the scooter.

"Look," Dolores says, pointing off into the distance. "There's a rainbow."

I look and look; she points some more. I crouch, squint, fail. "I don't think I see it."

"Right there." She points more adamantly, still speaking softly.

"I don't think that's a rainbow."

"It is, but it's very faint."

"Oh," I say, "I see it. There." It's a thin cloud, with weak sunshine behind it, and shaped like the McDonald's logo.

Back at the table, back at the tea, Dolores and I get to the only subject we have in common, my brother's ear bones.

"Do you ever get tired of people thanking you, for what your family did?"

Only a jerk would say yes.

"No. It was the best decision I have ever been a part of. And meeting people like your son only reinforces that feeling."

Don't thank me again, though.

"Thank you, Eric. I can't tell you what it has meant to us. Not so much because of the hearing issue itself. I mean, Philip doesn't even like music, for goodness' sake. But because . . . just life, you know? Living. Before, he wasn't part of things, wasn't getting along. Now he's just a lot more with us than before. His other ear's okay, not so great, but this has made a huge difference. Might need the other ear done someday."

"Well," I say, out of awkwardness or the spirit of Duane overcoming me, "I can't live forever, so we'll see."

Dolores gasps, covers her mouth with her hand, and backs away from me.

Whoops.

"I'm sorry, Dolores," I say.

She removes her hand to reveal a guilty toothy grin. "Oh, you are a rascal," she says, to my great relief.

"Thank you," I say. "But if you think I'm a rascal . . . my brother would have rascalled your eyebrows off."

"You mention him a great deal, still?" she says, a statement in a question.

"Yeah, I suppose I do," I say, staring into my tea. "Duane loved ginger."

Dolores giggles.

"I did it again, just there, didn't I?"

"Yes. But I know what it's like. Philip is like that about you."

This is only the second time we have met.

"What? He is? I mean, that's really nice. He is?"

Who are these people? To me? Who am I, to them?

"Don't be alarmed. He's not a stalker yet or anything."

Yet. His mother said "yet."

I hear the scooter approaching outside. I hop up and head for the window, happy for the momentary diversion. "Here they come," I say, watching them zip up the road toward us. They get closer, approach the house. And steam right on past.

Martha is driving.

"He is still very young," Dolores says as I stare longingly after the scooter fumes. "He never knew his father, and he's always been a little isolated, with his hearing issues. And I suppose I have sheltered him. I'm his best friend; that is without question."

In a fairly short time, she has got me following along with her story, feeling I almost know them now. Surely more than they could know me. I turn from the road to look at her as she talks, which is only polite.

She is beaming as she speaks of odd, endearing, red Phil.

"And then there's the hair thing," I say, and I swear I had no intention of saying anything like it. Dammit, Duane, cut it out.

"Well, it hasn't made it any easier, I can tell you that," she says, pointing to her own faded chopped strawberry locks. "So he has made, I think, something of a folk hero of you. Not unlike what you are doing, a little bit, with your brother."

"Hey," I say, indignant. But not. Folk hero.

I hear the motor approach from the other direction and turn just in time to see it disappear again, Martha whooping like a mad gal, and Phil matching her.

Dolores, suddenly behind me, squeezes both of my trapezius muscles, and I jump.

"Jeez," I say, turning to face her.

She takes both of my hands. "I know I shouldn't be here. Philip wouldn't know any better, but I do. I invited myself, because I wanted to see you, to thank you, and to tell you. About him, in a way he wouldn't have told you. That's all. When they get back, we will be on our way."

"Oh, no, no—"

"Shh. It's time. This has been a perfect day. A *perfect* day. Very few days turn out precisely the way you would want them to, so when you see one working out just like that, you shut your mouth and run before it falls down. Martha is a fine woman. You are a fine young man. I couldn't be more proud and pleased to have a piece of your family in my family."

Perfect.

"Well, it *did* rain—"

"Shush," she shushes.

Finally we hear the two motormouths scrambling up the

stairs, yakking away, laughing, bouncing helmets off the walls. They come through the door, ruddy-faced and bright-eyed.

"Well," Dolores says, "how was that?"

Phil tries to answer, but his hands, his mouth, his eyebrows, all look like they are taking instructions from different air traffic controllers, because all he can do is splutter and stammer and gesticulate nuttily.

"Beyond awesome," Martha says. "It was just like I had imagined, hoped it would be. Me and this dude . . . *dude*," she says, and squeezes Phil's shoulders together like playing an accordion. "We turned this sleepy drab town into Rome, is what we did. All by ourselves. Everything looked different, just like that. Everything, all the restaurants and alleys and train tracks, came closer, and faster, and more vivid—and in Italian—than I ever experienced before."

Phil is actually hugging himself from the thrill of it.

Dolores is this close to doing the same. They wear matching lighthouse-beam grins.

I stare at Martha as she continues, haltingly. I get the oddest conflicted sensation as she gives the oddest conflicted rendition.

She is smiling, broadly and luminously, while at the same time her bottom lip quivers uncontrollably. "Thank you so much," she says, suddenly grabbing Phil in a bear hug that could kill him if it didn't appear to be also giving him live-forever strength. "You're great. I am very happy to find that you are great."

"It's the other ear," he says.

"I know," she says. "You're great on both sides."

"It is time for us to go," Dolores says in a way most satisfied.

"What?" Phil says, looking every bit his age, minus some. He does everything but stomp his foot.

"Yes," is all his mother says, softly, but quite enoughly.

He's a good boy. He's the goodest boy.

Everybody thanks everybody a million times, and everybody tells everybody else they will be getting in touch and planning something else, and even as the words are out and floating there in the air and jumbling up like a fresh batch of Scrabble tiles, I have no idea if any of it means what it is supposed to.

Martha and I go to the window, balcony, and watch them mount up. We don't open the glass door, even though it is nicer outside now than it has been all day. Neither of us reaches for the door or mentions it.

The glass partition between in here and out there feels right.

They are both waving, Dolores like a queen, Phil like an excitable prince.

And it's Dolores's turn to drive.

"So?" I say as we stand there watching long after they have gone. At some point I seem to have slipped my arm around her waist. At some point she seems to have draped an arm across my shoulders. "Rome, huh?"

She shakes her head, whispers something I can't make out, and we watch the sky for whatever.

PIECES

"Who cares who *gets it*? It's like jerkin' off—as long as *you* get it, that's all that really matters."

GOOD GRIEF

I don't get it. Don't get them, really. My parents. I don't get
them and they don't get me, but mostly that's fine. Mostly
that's the way it's always been, mostly that's common for
families like us.

So what am I talking about? I'm talking about this new
thing, this ghostly thing that has been haunting us since
Duane died. I thought at first we had one ghost to deal with,
but now we have four. We see each other, in the kitchen, the
hall, the driveway, and we speak and all, but it is hollow, as
if the house is empty and the windows are all open a crack
and breezes just waft in and out, making only the lightest
sound and the faintest impact. We are ghosts passing through
ghosts, and the reason I don't get it is, well, he was mine.

He had little positive impact on their lives after the age
of, say, twelve—and, sorry, but people get over these things.
They do.

It's different for me. He was mine. I was his. He was live,
he was life.

I don't get it.

o o o

There's an extra layer to Martha now too, a level of something that I didn't detect before meeting Phil and Dolores. An unreachable something.

"Can't we just get him a card?" I ask as we stand in front of the window of the specialty kids' store. The place is cheery, bright, and colorful, and every toy and gadget looks like there will be an exam at the end of playing with it.

"Don't be a Philistine," she says.

I look at my reflection in the window, looking too stupid to have ever played with one of these smarty toys. "Are you gonna make me look that up?" I ask. "I'm sure there's a dictionary for toddlers in there someplace."

"It means, 'Have a little class, will ya?' This is a special boy; he gets a special gift."

She pushes through the doors, heads straight for a number of electronic keyboard contraptions.

"You think maybe we're taking this kinda fast, Martha? I mean, what if he turns out to be a brat, or a biter, or one of those kids who has his finger in his nose all the time?"

"He won't be any of that," she says.

I wait for the rationale while she plays something that sounds like the introduction to "A Whiter Shade of Pale" on the keyboard.

"Because?" I ask.

"This one is perfect," she says as she scoops up an unopened box, and we head to the checkout desk.

That's the kind of vision she seems to have now. Straight ahead, clear, periphery be damned.

"It's kind of a lot of money, especially for a kid we never even met yet," I suggest, noting the staggering range of products we could explore.

"Fine," she says. "Don't chip in."

"I didn't say . . ." I start fumbling all the cash out of my pocket as she takes out her wallet. "Jeez, Martha, relax."

"We are also going to be late."

"I don't think we are."

"I thought you wanted to do this, Eric?"

"I thought so too," I say. "But I thought we were two normal people going to a kid's birthday party, not the two wise men following a star."

She pays and takes the keyboard toward the exit.

"There were three wise men, dodo."

"Sheesh," I say, going ahead of her and holding the door, "this must be what it's like being married."

She stops as I hold the door, and pokes me in the chest. "Exactly what himself would have said."

This is it, you see, what she's done. Martha's brought the whole thing back, back out, back up, back in. I had to meet the recipients, just to get some idea of where Duane's pieces were, where they'd been, and where they might be going. I was trying to see if I could feel something just a little more than I was feeling, before Duane slipped further away from me. I think I was getting somewhere with that. But Martha coming back, and her not knowing, and her having to make her way through it, this is a massive rewind, reeling me back in too, and, I suppose, my parents.

The living dead, huh, D? You'd've liked that.

I am driving my parents' B-car the hour or so to where Melinda lives in New Hampshire. It's as old as me and was the no-frills model even when it was new, but we get along fine. It's a pleasant enough drive, though a little samey after the first three million billion pine trees and granite outcroppings. This doesn't seem to be a problem for Martha, who stares at it all in almost total mesmerized silence until we turn off the highway and start the winding wind-down part of the trip. She insisted I keep Dad's classical music station on the whole way, and by this time I am pretty sure that what made Mozart nuts was his own music.

I switch to the local station playing screamy metal rock, which I don't like but which at least gets her attention.

"I never liked it around here," she says, turning the radio down but not off or over to another station.

"You can change that," I say, laughing and pointing at the radio dial.

"Oh, no. I am a firm believer in 'When in Rome, do as the Romans do.'"

The music is actually making the whole experience of the area seem more grungy than necessary. It's not really a bad place so much as it is a non-place.

"Rome," Martha sighs, turning away and letting her head lean against the half-open window.

"Rome?" I ask, the metal thrash sifting softly through the air between us.

She doesn't give me anything, and I don't like it. I stare at the side of her head as she stares at poor southern New Hampshire, and I get a little angry. I feel like a kid again. Like I don't understand a thing, like everything is escaping me, and the loss of control over anything and everything hots up my face and my whole bloodstream.

Who are these people, Duane? Who are they? Who are the ghosts you left me with back home?

And who is this? With me here now?

I am still staring as it all comes apart.

Cuurrr-rasshh.

At a four-way intersection, I have smashed right into the back of a 4x4 pickup truck that must do a lot of off-roading, because there is mudsplash all over it, and it's raised up so high I can see the whole transmission. My dad's ancient midsize Ford has almost disappeared under the truck's rear end. We are actually lucky we didn't disappear right under that thing and wind up decapitated, it was that close.

Martha let out one ancestor-raising scream, and now is trying to disappear into the upholstery, her hands covering most of her face.

"You all right?" I ask her.

She remains frozen except for a micro-nod that is mostly brow.

"What the hell are you doin'?" comes the driver, screaming red-white-and-blue at me. He has long hair, a beard that covers only the round ball at the end of his chin. He wears a straw cowboy hat like most male country singers seem to wear, the front and back rims bent way low so his eyes are pretty well a mystery. His checkered button-down shirt has the sleeves cut off. He appears to work out. At his local tavern.

"I'm sorry, pal," I say, walking to the front of my car to inspect the crunch.

"I ain't your pal, blondie," he shouts from the other side of the crunch.

"Blondie?" I say, stunned. Then, "Okay. Great. Listen, it was my fault. But there doesn't seem to be—"

"It was *all* your fault," he bellows.

The force of his voice makes me blink, even from a distance.

"As I was saying," I say, "it looks like my car is the one with all the damage. So if you want, we'll just go—"

"We are exchanging papers, punk. You probably ain't even got a license." He suddenly looks into the passenger seat of my car, where the occupant has stirred slightly. Traffic is light and swerves around us without any rubbernecking, we are so ordinary.

He sticks his tongue out at Martha, which is rude. He was talking to me, after all.

"Hey," I say, demanding his attention.

He does a small snake-flick with his tongue in Martha's direction while he holds his genitals securely in place.

"Excuse me, Mr. Scumbucket," I yell across to him.

His head whips in my direction.

"Why don't you come around this way," I say, giving him the most punky, sleazy, come-here-bring-it-on motion I can conjure, using the ring and middle fingers of both hands to beckon him. "We'll exchange papers."

Just like that, he's got his skates on. He comes around to the sidewalk side of his huge machine, where we are shielded from the street's prying eyes.

"Listen, shithead," I say, "there was no need—"

Bam, I take one right in the mouth and reel backward about four feet.

It has been a while.

I gather my senses, plow forward, and in seconds it all comes back to me. With my left hand I grab his shirt, pull him toward me, *bang*, hit him in the mouth with my right, *bang*, hit him in the mouth. I keep a good grip on that shirt collar, drag him left, right, push him back, and all the while I wind-mill away with my right hand hitting him squarely on the nose, rattling some teeth, crack the left eye. When I hit him one last laser shot in the mouth, I am certain I feel teeth give way on the bottom row. Not so much that they fall out but that they are all still wobbling away in there as he tumbles backward and lands flat on his back.

The hat stays right in place. How do they do that?

I feel good. Later I expect to feel bad about feeling good. I hope that later I feel bad about feeling good. Right now, though, I'm going to feel good.

"Hey," I say, taking a slip of paper from my pocket. I lean down to his bruised and oozing face. "You're local, right? Where's this address?"

He may be trying to think, like you do when you know an address but as soon as somebody asks you, you go blank. Or he just may be blank. I don't have time to wait for him. I have a party to go to.

I turn from the man and am headed back to my car when I'm almost eyes-to-eyes with a little boy in a little cowboy hat, staring googly at me from the truck's passenger seat window.

We stare at each other for five seconds, and I feel the sick rising in my throat. The guy on the pavement sits up, starts gurgle-growling something, and I bolt.

I jump into the car and gun it in reverse, and there are hor-rible clawing, squealing metal noises from the front of the car. Then I haul us into traffic.

"I know what you did," Martha says coldly.

"Maybe you don't," I say.

She is shaking her head, a lot, I can see in my peripheral view, but I'm not going to look.

"I don't know what you think you are these days, but I'll tell you this, you're no Duane. He wouldn't have done *that*, I'll tell ya."

I grip the wheel, watch the road.

"Martha, could ya, just for a while, shut up about Duane?"

And I thought *my* family was good at silence.

We find the neighborhood, in silence, park the car, in silence, and now we stand in the little lobby of the little apartment building, in silence.

That little boy's face keeps insisting itself into my mind.

"What?" I say.

"What, yourself."

"What, you wanna just go home?"

"What, are you stupid? We come all the way to this god-awful place just so you can smash your car into some local, get into a fight that makes you feel like a big man, then come to the *lobby* of the place we were supposed to go to in the first place. Then we're gonna go home—with the pricey present we bought—without even seeing anybody?"

"I don't feel like a big man. At all. Besides, who said the present was too expensive? Huh? I did."

We stand there, glowering at each other. A couple, with a little boy, come through the lobby and look at us as if they're well aware we're bitching. We smile, wave, wait for them to pass, then go back to bitching.

"Still love me?" she snarls.

"Yes, I do," I snarl.

"Fine. Let's go up, then."

"Fine."

Again, I have the urge to make that just-like-married remark. This time I resist.

We knock at the door and wait. The apartment complex is connected by outside stairways that are clogged with bikes and baby carriages, milk crates stuffed with toys, and big plastic bags stuffed with who knows. Martha shrugs when we get no answer despite there being a few voices inside and a little music. So I try the knob, and we're in.

There are four tykes—three boys and a girl—and two women standing in the combination kitchen–living room. As we step in, one of the moms walks away from the other, past us, and out the door. Then Melinda comes rushing our way.

"Eric," she says with enough excitement in her voice to make my stomach flutter.

She gives me a big hug, which I enjoy. Then she turns to Martha. I introduce them, and Melinda proceeds to give Martha just as big a hug.

"I am so, so glad you guys could come," Melinda says. The little white Highland terrier comes shuffling over to us, and Martha crouches down to pet him. "I've been telling Dean about you, and about Duane and all of it, and I think he just about gets it. At any rate, it thrills me, to have family here for him. Hold on just a second," she says, walking quickly off to another room.

I watch Melinda walk.

"Hey," Martha says, still crouched. I look down to see her grinning slyly at me.

"What?" I ask.

"You pervin' on her?"

"I am not . . . I'm not *pervin'* on anyone. Don't be gross."

She laughs. "Well, if you don't, I will."

Oh, my. I don't like to be too shocked by things ordinarily, but before I can get ahold of it, a small gasp escapes me. This makes Martha giggle.

"Don't be such a prude, Eric."

"Um, y'know . . . I would think, maybe at least out of respect for my brother, your—"

"Pffft," she sprays. "Are you kidding? Your brother would so approve. Right now he's up there, or down there, cheering, with pom-poms and high kicks and everything."

I've never been to a children's birthday party before. This is not how I imagined one to be.

"Stop that now," I say.

She sees my discomfort, which only ups the ante.

"You didn't know this about your brother? I thought guys always bragged about sex stuff—and, boy, he had plenty to brag about."

"Stoppp iiiit." My words drag like they are carrying too heavy a load.

"I mean, sure, on a Friday he was a romantic . . . but by Sunday it was pure terrorism. Bless his smudgy soul."

She is laughing heartily by the time she gets to the last part, and I know she is trying to freak me out, but she *is* freaking me out. And I know this kind of naughty nudge is good for her, good for us, in a tribute-to-Duane kind of way. But . . . it's a lot of things, all mashing up together in entirely the wrong combinations. I don't need to hear about this side of my brother, or this side of Martha, for that matter. When I was a kid, I might have worshipped her, a little, in *that* way . . . but now, romancing Lady Duane would feel about as appropriate as swapping limericks with my father.

And I really don't need to feel *anything* about the mother of the birthday boy, or to think, even for one more second about . . .

I beat up a guy, right in front of his little boy. Duane could stretch that stretchy moral code of his in every which way, but I know he would kill me for that.

I would kill me for that.

"This is Dean," Melinda says, suddenly reappearing, standing behind the guest of honor with her hands clamped onto his rounded little shoulders.

"Oh, my," Martha says, leaving the dog for now, but remaining on her knees, approximately the boy's height. She shakes his hand. "I have seen your picture a lot, Dean, but I have to say, like with most movie stars, you're much more handsome in person."

Dean leans heavily backward into his mother, his face going a rosy pink.

"Hi, Dean," I say, bending down to shake his hand. "Happy Birthday."

"Hello," he says, and gives my hand the grip of somebody three times his weight. There are lots of boys who try hard to do that with men. I know. But this isn't that. There is no special effort behind this grip.

"Holy smokes," I say, "do you lift a lot of weights? You're strong."

"You're not strong," he says. "My dad's a lot stronger than you."

"Oh, Dean," laughs Melinda, "let's not bring your father's smell into it."

We laugh, but Martha shoots me an unsure look.

"Here you go," Melinda says, producing what she apparently went to the other room to retrieve.

"Party bags?" Martha says.

"Party bags for party guests," Melinda chirps.

"Oh, really," I say, "you don't have to. Save these for the other—"

"This is it. It's okay. We have plenty. We were expecting a few more. Guess they couldn't come," Melinda says.

"Guess they couldn't come," her son echoes.

"With the no-shows, we are extra glad you're here," Melinda says, and there is no doubt from her demeanor that she means it. "Enjoy."

She twirls around toward the other kids and claps her hands, rounding them up.

I look into my bag. It contains a pink candy lipstick, a single baseball card, a plastic key chain with a mini soccer ball attached, and some loose jelly candies. Martha looks into her bag, takes out one candy, smiles, and closes the bag back up again.

"Chuck E. Cheese! Chuck E. Cheese!" Melinda chants, leading a conga line of kids to the door.

"Oh," I say as they pass us by, "the party's not here?"

She turns to the kids. "Kids?"

"Chuck E. Cheese! Chuck E. Cheese!"

Having made their point, the conga line continues to and through the door.

"I guess we're going to Chuck E. Cheese," Martha says.

"What's Chuck E. Cheese?" I ask.

She shakes her head in despair at my cluelessness.

○ ○ ○

The first thing one notices about the place is the noise. It is a pure wall of sound, of screaming kiddie voices and music and some sort of cartoon-character silliness weaving through and rising above it all. It makes me chuckle even as we cross the lot from the car to the entrance.

Once there, we are reunited with the other members of our party and head inside. There, the next big thing you notice is the security.

"Right," the entrance girl says, counting heads and sizing us up. "You, right? And you and you and you."

They check to be certain who has come in together, because that's who will be leaving together. No funny business when Chuck E. is on the case. A kid comes in with his people and leaves with his people and with nobody else. And his people, his tribe, is defined by the stamp.

"Right," she says again. "You, and you, and you." Only this time each "you" is accompanied by a luminous hand stamp, with our team number on it. We are seventeen. All of us, for this day, are the seventeen family in the land of Cheese.

I like it.

"I like it," Martha says. "Makes sense. Cool," she says, rolling her fist around under the flashing lights to catch all the sparkle of the occasion.

And from this point the kids rule. Dean and his pals hit the accelerator, and we all follow like the tail of a comet, into the bleeping and squealing madness of the place.

It is like every carnival I have ever seen, every arcade, every midway, and a little bit of Disney World thrown in. There are ancient games like Skee-Ball, flight simulators, Whac-A-Mole, flashing dance floor things, and in a corner a weirdly sad collection of giant animatronic musicians that spark to life every few minutes to put on a bit of a musical floor show that is actually shocking in that it does not scare the pants off every little party animal here. It gives me the chills.

"That's Chuck himself right there," Martha calls into my ear.

"The host is a giant rat," I say.

"Come on, he's a mouse."

"Hey, I used to feed rodents to my reptiles, and *that* is a rat. A rat that is bigger than me, I might add."

And there is no avoiding the obvious as Martha and I both jump to say what Duane would have said.

"There is no rat bigger than you!"

We high-five and laugh as much as the kids, and Melinda comes right up to us.

"What? What is it?" she asks. "You're having more fun than they are."

Martha tells her, and they both do that head-tilt thing that means *awww* in the best possible way.

"Did you love him?" Melinda asks. "I mean, really *love* him?"

Martha nods, the corners of her mouth pilling downward.

"Want to feel his kidney?" Melinda asks. "For old time's sake?"

"Bye," I say, waving frantically and heading for the more wholesome fun of the kiddies. If my system encounters any more such powerful mixed signals, it's gonna crash.

"Hey," I say, coming up to Dean as he shoots out the end of a tube slide.

"Hey," he says, acknowledging me and ignoring me at the

same time. I follow along as he leads his little group from the slide, to a motorcycle simulator, to air hockey. He tries several games that require the special Chuck E. Cheese gold token coin even though he has no tokens. He jumps on, simulates simulation, then goes on to the next thing. I look back to see the women sitting at a booth about twenty yards away deep in conversation, but still watching us. They both wave. I wave back. I suppose I have nominated myself as designated monitor, but that's fine with me.

In fact, I get a small thrill when I realize that, every couple of minutes, Dean is checking over his shoulder to see that I am still there.

I have never felt anything like this. How do I explain this to anyone? How do I explain it to myself?

I tag along, watching the kids have loads of fun doing not much else but pinging around the place like pinballs. Then I pass a counter selling the gold tokens, and quickly, without losing visual contact with my pod, I buy a batch.

"Here," I say, catching them just as they pass the Skee-Ball. I work coins into all the four-year-old mitts, and feel again the rush of whatever—power, love, domination, control, I don't know. I do know I am right now as popular as I have ever been in my life.

Then, when they pump the coins and start slinging balls at the targets, the real payback begins. Each minor success produces results as the machine spits out tickets, which can later be turned in for indescribably cheap-looking prizes. The tickets themselves probably have more intrinsic value than the toys they will be exchanged for, but no matter, no matter at all.

The four kids huddle, comparing modest ticket tallies, then turn to wave them in my face.

We all whoop and celebrate, and I feel like I have won an election in Munchkinland or something.

"Hey," I say, tapping Dean on the shoulder as they run toward the next thing.

He stops, practically jogging in place as he looks up at me.

"Play some air hockey?" I ask hopefully.

"No," he says as quickly as a person can say a syllable. And he is off like a pinball again.

I follow along, feeling myself grin. I watch the four of them do some more Skee-Ball, try this simulator and that game of skill, stop to watch the spooky rat-infested animatronic floor show. Then, they return once more to their real passion—games that produce those tickets.

Until finally they run out of tokens. Then I get all kinds of popular again.

"Please, please, please, please," they chant as a group, a mob really, and I don't have the heart to say no. *How do parents do this?* I wonder. How do you say no? How do you keep from going broke? How do you not become addicted to this tre-mendous feeling of . . . awesomeness that comes with pleas-ing these happy noisy mites.

"No," Melinda says from suddenly right next to me.

So that's how it's done.

"Thank you very much, Eric," she says, sounding like a schoolteacher. "What do you say to Eric, kids?"

"Thank you, Eric."

It is a much more deflated sound than they were making at me before. But then an employee comes to Melinda and whispers into her ear, and we all march over to the great and magical tube of wonders.

What it is is an enclosed glass cylinder, which the birthday boy walks into like a closet. It is then closed, a switch is flipped, and air jets shoot upward inside, spraying the cherished tickets in a mad upward blizzard—and shocking everybody in the vicinity. Dean, for his part, starts jumping up and down like he is spring-loaded, his little hands grabbing tickets out of the air like his hands are covered in glue. Every kid in the place has gathered like it's a school-yard fight except with less violence, and we all cheer him on for the full sixty seconds of the most mercenary minute of any boy's life.

It is, apparently, a Chuck E. Cheese birthday party tradition. And I have to give the giant rodent credit this time.

And by the time it's done, I realize my heart has been racing and I have drilled four fingernail dents into the palm of each of my hands by mime-grabbing along with Dean the whole way.

He steps out of the machine like a triumphant astronaut returning to Earth. The group regain their power, spin, and run right to the ticket redemption booth. Within minutes their faith is rewarded, having exchanged the tickets for stunning prizes. The little girl has a small notebook and pen combo, as well as a deck of playing cards, all bearing the likeness of Chuck E. Cheese. The two other boys have a pair of fuzzy dice and a baseball-size basketball, also Chuck-bearing. Dean comes away with the biggest haul of all, naturally, a stuffed Chuck doll roughly the same size as Dean's dog, wearing a sweater with the big C on its chest and his mouth open crazy-way-wide. And as he's walking away from the counter, who comes along but the big Cheese himself, marker in hand to sign it.

Does life get any better on a guy's birthday? I don't suppose it does.

"Pizza!" Melinda calls, and the kids are airborne with delight as she leads them back toward the booth.

"Um," I say, holding up my one remaining gold token. "Dean, wouldja play one game of air hockey with me now?"

"Sure," says Dean, feeling flush with success and goodwill toward men.

"Okay," Melinda says, while Martha chatters away with the other three, "but come right over afterward before the pizza gets cold." She takes the doll for safekeeping.

I can't remember the last time I played air hockey, but it really doesn't matter. It's a fun game to play whether you're any good at it or not, which is a good thing, since within a few seconds I am down two-to-nothing to a four-year-old. And I'm trying.

"You're good," I say.

"Yeah," he says, concentrating fiercely.

Two-to-one. He's not pleased with this development. "You're not my dad."

I am both stunned and amused. More stunned.

"I understand that."

"Who are you?"

So now he is defeating me at the hockey and the quiz.

"A friend of your mom's?" I say with a half spin too much of honest confusion. "Is it okay for me to be your friend?"

Pause.

Three-to-one.

"Yes," he says triumphantly.

We play out the rest of the game, full speed and full effort, and the lad wins four-to-two. This is a good result that leaves us both satisfied. Almost.

"Can you get more coins?" he asks.

"Uh, your mom said we have to go back to the table now. C'mon, before the pizza gets cold."

We get back, and the pizza is going down a storm all around when we join in.

"This is surprisingly good," Martha says into my ear as I sit next to her.

"I'm glad," I say into her ear. "And how's the pizza?"

Across the way, Melinda is smiling at us knowingly. Not sure what it is she is knowing, but it's beautiful. She is also being attentive to her son, making sure that he gets some of each of the three kinds of pizza she's ordered, and that his guests are happy too.

"It's a hard job," Martha says, acknowledging the mothering. "I don't know if I could do it, ever."

"Sure you could," I say.

She goes quiet for a bit.

"We talked about it," she says, nodding.

I go quiet for a bit. Nephews, nieces.

"I think maybe I'd be a better father than I ever was a son," I say.

Suddenly there is a commotion at the front desk. The gatekeepers seem all aflutter about somebody there attempting to violate their security setup. A man is there, pointing in this general direction, getting a lot of "No, no" answers. He starts pointing at the back of his hand, like he wants what we have, stamp-wise.

Melinda swivels around in her booth to look back over her shoulder.

"Ah, Jesus," she says. "Sorry, but could you guys keep an eye on things here while I go see to this?" she says, and there is no time for answers as she is up and scurrying to the scuffle.

"Right," Martha says, getting all the kids' attention going her way. She snaps up the deck of playing cards and starts shuffling, chattering like a carnival barker as she does. "Who's gonna cut first, who's the luckiest, who's . . . Oh, silly me, it's the birthday boy, of course."

Good timing, as Dean was just about getting his head turned all the way around to look at the distant action when she called him to cut the cards. I'm not sure what the kids believe the payoff is going to be, but they keep cutting in turn with such enthusiasm that either they think it's more coins or more tickets or they are just so competitive, it doesn't even matter. At any rate, Martha's instincts are good.

I am much more interested in what is going on at the entrance, where Melinda has gone back out through the high-security gate and confronted the man. She has taken custody of him from the workers and has backed him up masterfully toward the door. There, however, a discussion is happening, and even through the distance and with all the other mayhem, I can see it is what we would call *heated*.

The man is comfortably over six feet tall, lean, and with salt-and-pepper hair. He and Melinda take turns pointing vigorously at each other while speaking so rapid-fire that it seems unlikely either one could possibly be hearing the other.

"I think I'm gonna go over there," I say.

"I think if you don't, I will," Martha says coolly, continuing her diversion.

"Are you gonna say that to everything now?" I say as I slip out of the booth.

I proudly show my number seventeen stamp to the woman at the gate as I step through. It's about another ten feet to the bit of wall where Melinda is arguing with the man. He sees me coming before she does.

"Goin' a little young this time, even for you, aren't ya, Mel?" he says, grinning at me.

Melinda turns around. "Eric, this doesn't concern you. Go back with the kids, please."

"Are you all right?" I ask, because I'm not going anywhere if she isn't.

"Yes. Now please—"

"You gonna introduce me, or what?" the man asks. He doesn't really expect an answer, as he makes an obvious and dramatic reach over Melinda's shoulder to shake my hand.

His right forearm has an elaborate tattoo of what appears to be Melinda's face.

"Eric," he says, smiling, "I'm Reg. I'm Dean's daddy, only I can't be at his party 'cause I don't got one of them seven-teens like you got there on your hand. Maybe if we just rub the back of our hands together, yours'll come off and mine'll come on and the world will be back the way it should be, like a kind of magic."

There seems little chance of that happening anytime soon, as Reg is absolutely crushing my hand in his. He keeps going up on his toes, looking over me to the booth where Dean is.

"He doesn't want you here, Reg," Melinda says.

"Let him tell me that, then."

"I'm not gonna let you spoil his day."

"So you're gonna let me in after all."

"Listen, it seems like this isn't gonna get you anywhere," I say, finally working my hand out of his grip. "So instead of this getting all weird and unpleasant, why don't you just go?"

Reg looks at me, tilting his head slightly as if trying to figure if I'm joking with him or what. Then he looks to Melinda, who stares back at him, expressionless.

"Go play with the other kids, kid, and let the adults talk. *Now*."

Melinda whips her head in my direction as if something horrific has just happened.

"It's okay, Eric. I can sort this out."

"That's right," Reg says, tapping me oh so lightly on the chest with his middle finger. Then he turns to Melinda and does the same thing. "Where were we," he says to her.

"You have to go, is where we were. I am here, Dean is there, and you are there," she says, pointing to herself, then her son, then the door. "That's where we are."

"Only way I'm going out that door is if my son is coming with me. You've had him long enough already. Let me take him someplace for his birthday now."

"He's not going with you," she says coolly.

He pauses, smirks, looks Melinda up and down, then leans closer to her. "Maybe you should come with me, then."

She freezes. I heat up.

"I'll come with you," I say.

"Well," Reg says, moving sideways toward the door, "startin' to look like it's *my* birthday."

I follow him out with my collection of conflicts swirling and expanding in my head. I know as I have this feeling that it is all wrong, but it doesn't slow the feeling down one little bit. Somehow, it's like, *Hey, I know. If I beat up this kid's rotten father for the right reasons and out of view of the kid, it somehow balances out my beating up the other kid's rotten father for iffy reasons right in front of the kid's eyes.*

There it is, a kind of chivalry with a cowboy boot up its ass.

"So," I say as I follow him out the door, into the sunny day, around the corner to the small side parking lot. "Did you say you were Melinda's dad?"

He turns around with something unclear on his lean grim face, but that thing is certainly not admiration.

"Son," he says slowly, "this is a textbook example of wrong time, wrong place, gettin' cute with the *wrong* guy."

I smile, but I do not feel like smiling. "Well, at least you've recognized your mistake. That's a start."

He raises his hands, as a matter of, I guess courtesy.

I raise mine. It doesn't matter. They could be in my pockets for all the good they do.

I don't see his left hand, it moves so quickly. Pop. He sticks me, hard, right in the cheek. I cover up, and he nails me in the ribs, the left kidney, the right kidney. I drop my hands, which he is waiting for, and pop, pop, he sticks me twice more, left cheekbone, right eye socket, and I go down.

If he wanted to stomp me, really mess me up, this is where he could do it. He prefers to just stand over me. I look up, and I am pretty certain his two feet are planted precisely where they were when he first raised his fists. No footwork required.

"These are the lessons of youth, young man. Learn. You do not come between a man and his family. Got that?"

I just look up at him, the sun bright behind him burning my eyes and making me tear up, which isn't helping me any, toughness-wise.

"Good," he says. "Now, out of respect"—he looks around, at the place—"for Chuck E. Cheese and his good work, I'm gonna do the gracious thing and leave for now. You tell Melinda I said she *needs* to call me. Right?"

I can't take the sun anymore, look down at the ground.

"Right?" he snaps.

"Right," I say.

I am almost thankful for the precision of Reg's fist work as I reenter the place, show them my seventeen, and head for the booth with my head down. My guts feel well pulped, my ribs creak like un-oiled hinges, and I can see my cheekbone rising like raw dough in front of my eye. But mostly I am not a mess—to the untrained four-year-old eye.

"Oh, my," Melinda says, reaching across to gently stroke my cheek, and that almost makes it all worthwhile.

I manage as cool as I can manage. "Ah, Reg would like you to give him a call. When you get a chance."

"Haven't you had a big busy day. Good Lord, knuckle-head," Martha says from right next to me. "What is *wrong* with you?" She elbows me fairly sharply in the ribs. A small groan comes out of me.

"I don't think I was at fault this time," I say.

It is fair to conclude that Martha is under-impressed.

"Maybe you really should go back to carrying around a big stick," she says.

The kids have finished their pizza, and stare at me over the crusts. The playing cards are spread out all over the table.

Chuck comes to the rescue, as he surely always does.

"Happy birth-day to you . . . Happy birthday to you . . ."

A team of waitstaff that outnumbers our whole party is singing, trailing behind Chuck E., who carries the cake with the four candles. We join in the singing, then most of the crowd joins in.

Dean, I see, is ecstatic. His mother, I see, is ecstatic. I sing my best and forget the rest, as everything else is gone, gone away.

"Moron," Martha growls into my ear as Dean blows out the candles and we all applaud.

"Do come back to the house," Melinda implores us as we stand in the parking lot. She has just packed the gifts away in the trunk. Dean is saying good-bye to his pals as their parents strap them into their seats. One of the fathers is definitely giving me a wary look.

"We should go," Martha says. "I'm sure the little guy has had all the excitement he can handle for one day."

"Oh, he can handle a fair bit of excitement," Melinda says. "He's got a high excitement threshold, I can assure you."

Dean rambles over and wraps an arm around his mother's leg. "What's wrong with your face?" he asks, pointing at my eye.

If you only knew about the ribs, I think.

"Bee sting," I say. "I'm allergic to bees."

"I hate bees," he says, nodding.

"Me too," I say.

"Please, do come back. Just for a glass of wine. I feel so bad." She reaches out both hands, taking one of Martha's hands and one of mine. "He's dying to play his amazing keyboards, aren't you, Dean?"

"Yesss," he says.

She had us with the hand-holding. No offense, Dean.

I don't really care much for wine, but the bright pink stuff Melinda serves us is cold and light and summery enough to make it nicely drinkable. I sip slowly, watching the boy play his keyboards and listening to two really lovely women chat. This, I figure, is more like what a fine summer day should be like.

"Reg couldn't really take it anymore, especially when my health was acting up at its worst," Melinda says. "He is not a truly bad guy. . . ." She trails off as if maybe one of us is supposed to finish the thought for her. "Ironically, if it was just me and him, and it wasn't so complicated and confusing for the sprout, we maybe could see how it goes again. But it's just too hard."

"Well," Martha says, "it seems to me like you have done an amazing job on your own. You should be proud, honestly." She raises a glass to the single mother, and they both drink up.

"Drink up," Melinda says to me as she hustles to the kitchen and comes back unscrewing the top from a fresh pink bottle.

"Oh, I would," I say, covering my half-full glass with my number seventeen hand, "but I have a long drive. Thanks, though." I stare at the stamp, which oddly thrills me.

The ladies drink a little more and become faster friends. The TV is on some old Western film, which has caught Dean's tired attention. He stares at it, sitting on the rug and occasionally plunking keyboard keys. He tips over sideways onto a throw pillow.

Melinda's phone goes off.

"I know," she says. "Yes, he told me. I was going to . . . No. No. No, I said. I am busy right now."

I look at Martha as Melinda gets up and walks the perimeter of the room, talking. Martha dramatically arches both eyebrows.

"No," Melinda says. "Don't do that. Right, right, all *right*."

She hangs up, comes over, and sits down close next to Martha.

"Listen, the thing is, he's outside. I don't want him coming up here. So, would you mind a lot, just hanging out for a few with Dean? He's wrecked. He'll probably sleep anyway. . . . Just for a few ticks?"

"Of course not," Martha says, sounding enthusiastic and tentative both. "Do what you need to do. We'll be here."

"You are a love," she says, kissing Martha. Then she comes over and kisses me. "Dolls."

She kisses Dean on the side of his head and disappears out the door without him appearing to notice much.

"Well," Martha says when she's gone.

"Well," I say. "I guess we are babysitters now."

"Aunt Martha and Uncle Eric," she says, getting up and pouring herself another glass of wine.

"Hmmm," I say, turning to the movie. I glide down from my chair to the floor, placing my glass on the coffee table.

"You mind if I come down here with you?" I say to Dean, taking a space on the rug about a foot away.

He shakes his head.

It is all-Western day on this station. The movie ends and another begins, and I could not have told you they were different films if I hadn't witnessed the credits in between. The sun then sets on that movie and comes up on a third as the sun coming in the window here disappears altogether. I must have nodded off at least briefly, because I hear the door close and then see Melinda hovering.

"Awww," she says.

Dean and I are both lying on our sides, facing the television, but stretched out in opposite directions. I feel the top of his little warm birthday head touching the top of my own foolish dome. Make that the top of *yesterday's* birthday head.

"Thank you *so* much," Melinda says, scooping him up. He is boneless and looks like he weighs a thousand pounds. I lie there following her with my eyes only.

I don't like the way she smells. I don't like the way she looks. I don't like the way she carries my little pal.

"Thank you *so* much," she says again, and I don't like at all the way she says it. "I owe you guys big-time," she says, the little man draped over her shoulder as she heads into the other room. "See you soon," she says, before closing the door behind her.

I sit up, look around this strange place. I go to the window, look around this strange place.

I turn off the TV and go to where Martha is asleep on the couch. The dog is nestled in with her.

"Hey," I say, "c'mon. We've been dismissed."

She looks up at me, blinks about a hundred times, then extends a hand. I pull her to her feet, and we take the first steps of the trip home.

I've been in two fights and one car accident since this trip began, but only now do I feel like I really hurt.

PIECES

"I don't believe in ghosts, because I don't believe they believe in me."

REMOTE CONTROL

"What happened to my car, Eric?"

There is a voice coming from the other side of my bedroom door.

I am waking from the depth of sleep. The kind of sleep that makes death jealous.

First I have to work out the voice, then figure out what this car business is.

Oh, Dad. Oh, Dad's *car*.

"Right. Oh, jeez, Dad. Right. Sorry. Somebody must have backed into me. When it was parked. It was all gouged up when I came out."

He waits. "Came out of where?"

"Chuck E. Cheese."

Now I wait. I eventually hear his slippered feet shuffle-padding down the hallway. He doesn't even ask. Must think I'm dinking on him.

I feel bad if he thinks that, that he would possibly think that.

I don't do anything about it though, do I?

And I know my car keys will no longer be hanging on the hook by the door downstairs. Access denied.

My phone message signal beeps.

"I have decided to forgive you."

Crap. It's Barry. I ignore him. He ignores my ignoring him. He beeps again.

"You went to Chuck E. Cheese with Mummy B. Yummy and didn't invite me?"

I can't ignore this. "Who told you that?"

I can just about hear him laughing. "Duane did."

Some things simply demand the personal touch, and text won't do.

"Hey, man," he sounds sickeningly chirpy.

"Knock it off, Barry, or I'm gonna break your skull."

"Hey, are we forgetting that *I* am the one who's been insulted and left out of parties and barbecues, and orgies, and that I should be the one offended? And I'm not, so maybe you should take my lead. You know, the *high road*."

"Who told you? And don't say Duane again, or I'm gonna kill you."

"Duane."

"Rrrrrr!"

"Oh, calm down. First, you're not gonna kill me. Second, how you gonna kill me? We're not even in the same place. You got a death ray or something? Because unless you have a death ray or something—"

"Who told you where I was? Barry, I mean it. If you don't stop messing with me . . ."

His voice downshifts right out of the amusement range.

"Stop threatening me. And get a grip on yourself. You're losing it, you know that? You need guidance. I knew that from the day I met you. You need me."

"I need you, to stop being a freak."

I may well have achieved a first, as I have gotten Barry to hang up on me.

I like the silence. I like the satisfaction. I would like to know how he got his information . . . but not as much as I presently like silence and satisfaction.

I lie back and stare at the ceiling. I raise my hand and examine the seventeen stamp once more with pride.

The doorbell rings downstairs. Not likely for me. Not interested, anyway.

Phone beeps. I sigh. "Creep," I say out loud, then check the message. It's from Melinda. Not interested in her right now either.

There is a knock at my door. "Dad, I will get the car fixed myself. Even though it was not my fault." When did I learn to lie so easily?

"It's not your dad. It's me, Phil."

I stare up at, and through, the ceiling. "Think this is funny, do ya?" I wonder if Duane can direct all his constituent parts like remote control cars.

"Come in, Phil."

Phil comes in, smiling. He's wearing long red shorts and a red-and-white checked shirt to go with the color scheme of his body and hair. In an old movie Phil's ghost would be played by someone wearing a table cloth from an Italian restaurant. He's doing his mad little wave with one hand and offering me a Tupperware soup container with the other. "Hi."

"Hi. How did you find my house, Phil?"

"Martha told me."

Jeez, Martha.

"And how did you get ahold of Martha?"

"I didn't. She called us. To thank us for coming to her indoor barbecue. Which was really nice and I think unnecessary, since it's probably the guests who should do the thanking, according to my mom. We would have called you anyway, because my mom did want to thank Martha, but we didn't have her number so I was planning to get it from . . ."

I see you there, Duane. Enjoy it while you can.

"Phil?"

"Yeah?"

"What's with the Tupperware?"

"I'm returning it."

"There's no need to return it, since it belongs to you. You brought soup in it, remember?"

"Ha," he says. "Funny thing, but I took the wrong one. See, blue, with a green top? Well ours was green, with a blue top. Funny, huh? Unless you're my mom, who doesn't think it's funny."

"You could have kept it. They all hold soup, don't they?"

"Right, unless you are my mom, with a full set of Tupperware that has green bottoms and blue tops. Right?"

I'm pretty sure that Tupperware salespeople don't talk Tupperware with as much gusto as this.

"Well, it's not even my Tupperware. It's Martha's."

"Oh. Can I leave it with you? Then I can collect ours next time."

Next time.

"Yes, you can leave it— Hold on. How did Martha get your number to call you?"

"She said she got it out of your phone."

"Out of *my* . . ."

Balls. Balls and balls again.

"Martha, my dear."

"Yes, Eric."

"I have Phil here. And your Tupperware."

"Oh, the green over blue. Good."

"Is it? Huh. And you got his number out of my phone?"

"You do just leave it lying around all over the place."

"Get any other numbers out of my phone while you were in there?"

She giggles.

"Martha?"

"Listen, I told you I wanted to meet them all."

"Oh, Martha."

"I think it's very funny you have him listed as Barry Beelzebub."

"That's because he is the devil!" I snap, which makes Martha laugh harder, but closer to hand, Phil is sort of cowering behind the Tupperware.

"Just calm yourself," Martha says. "I had to do it because you were never going to make it happen, on account of your bizarre protectiveness-possessiveness thing, which, by the way, I think is making you slightly violently crazy at the moment."

"Hah," I laugh the pathetic laugh of the soundly defeated. "I guess the only thing to say to that is, good-bye, Martha."

"That's not the only thing," she says. "I could think of several choice—"

I cut her off before she can get to them. I dial, God help me, Barry.

"Y'know," he says, a little out of breath, "you're getting to be kind of a nuisance here, Eric. I've got a life beyond you."

"You've got a life *because* of me," I growl. "Sort of."

Phil rather wisely takes this as the moment to start miming and bowing his exit. He places the Tupperware in the middle of my floor like a bomb and starts backing away. I wave at him, *Thanks*.

"Point taken," Barry says. "Now, as you and me and Duane can all agree, I should be making a point of doing something with that life. Am I right?"

"Of course." Of course he's right. Even Barry is allowed that.

"Or doing some*one* with that life, right? Eric, can I get an amen?"

"Barry?"

"Eric?"

I am causing him to enjoy this far too much, and must figure out a way to stop. But I can't.

"Where are you now, Barry?"

"Of all people, you have to agree that Duane would approve, huh?"

"Stop saying his name, Barry, please."

"Stop saying my name, Barry, please."

"Where *are* you?"

I hear Phil's scooter engine revving outside. I go to the window, and he's already looking up, waving at me. He's fiddling with this and that, extending his "visit." He is lovable, in a don't-know-if-I-could-stand-it kind of a way.

"I think I'm about a block away from heaven. Just tell me," Barry says, and I am starting to wonder about the cause of the breathlessness, "is she as hot as she sounds? Just tell me that. Not that it's gonna make a difference to me at the end of the day anyway—"

"Phil!" I holler out the window just as he is pulling away from the curb. He stops short right in the middle of the street, yanks off his helmet, and cups his bad ear at me. "Don't go away! Wait right there. I'm coming down."

"Phil?" Barry harrumphs. "Phil is there? You invite *that* weenie over to your house, and I don't even—"

I hang up on a moderately high note. Score one for ol' Phil.

"What happened to your face?" he asks as I strap on the helmet.

"Exactly the same thing that's gonna happen to yours if—" I stop myself when I see him flinching in the face of my nastiness. I grab his arm and give it a calming squeeze. "Sorry, Phil. It's a bee sting. I'm allergic to bees."

"Hey, my mom has something she makes up for bee stings. You want to maybe swing by there—"

"This way, Phil. Please. No time for side trips."

It takes us about ten minutes to weave our way through traffic over to Martha's apartment. This is not a style of driving my man is used to, as he keeps making small *whoo* noises, both worried and thrilled, while I drive him on like a jockey at the whip.

Standing at the door, I keep buzzing Martha's apartment, with no answer. It is a beautiful sunny day, so when I do hear her distinctive throaty laugh, I zip around to the building's communal backyard.

"Hey," I call when I see them. They are sitting on two folding lounge chairs, the kind with the plastic-fabric weave. They are facing each other with a rock like a giant tortoise between them supporting their bare feet. "Hey, what is this?"

"This"—Barry holds a up a two-liter pitcher full of thick red with a celery stalk protruding—"is bloody Martha."

Martha raises her glass. In the other hand she's holding a burning cigarette.

"You don't smoke," I say.

"I think you're mistaken there, dude," Barry says. Then he sees my accomplice coming into the yard in his red-and-white checkerboard shirt. "We'll have the fried calamari and a coupla calzones, waiter."

Martha laughs.

"That's not funny," I say.

"I think you're mistaken again there, dude."

"Shut up, you."

"He's very tense," Barry says to Martha.

"Yes, he is. Eric, you really need to calm yourself, or you can just leave again. I don't know what your problem is, anyway."

"My problem—" I announce.

And I stop, dead, right there. Because really I don't know how to finish.

What I have managed to do is silence the crowd. Everybody is waiting for me to finish, or at least add a little something. I'm waiting for it myself. But it doesn't come.

"Have a bloody," Barry says, waving me over.

"Why?" I say, but I come to the beckoning hand as if I were attached to it by fishing line.

"Because it's still morning," he says.

I come to them, but decline the drink. I sink into the grass beside Martha's chair, resting my hand on her armrest. She covers my hand with hers.

"Sorry," Phil says to her. "I forgot your Tupperware. I left it over at Eric's house. You want me to go get it?"

"No, not necessary. I'll just keep yours as a hostage for the time being. You're a love, though."

He goes all blushy. Phil sits alongside Barry's chair, parallel with what I am doing, and an odder couple there has probably never been. Barry simply stares down at him as if he's some sort of red meteor that just fell from the sky. The powerfully sunny sky.

"Aren't you going to burn?" Martha asks Phil with real concern.

"It's a distinct possibility," Phil says.

"Burn?" says Barry with nothing at all like real concern. "He's gonna burst into flames."

"I'll go get some sunscreen," she says, and scoots to her apartment.

"Factor infinity," Barry calls after her. He turns back around to regard the remaining group. "I guess you're wondering why I gathered you all here today."

"Nobody's wondering that," I say.

"I kind of am, now that you mention it," says Phil.

"The truth is, I would appreciate it if you guys would buzz off now. We're all men of the world. You see what I got on the line here."

"You have nothing on the line," I say. "Can't you just, for a few minutes, drop that and stop being a dirtbag? Just for a few minutes?"

"Why would I do that? The babe loves me just the way I am."

"Grrrr," I say.

"Jeez, I hate when you do that growling thing, Eric," Martha says, marching back across the grass. "Honestly, you sound like some kind of animal." She grabs Phil's arm—a little roughly, which is my fault—and stares my way as she applies sun cream. He stares up at her, smiling stupid puppy loving all over her. She looks like she's a nurse swabbing his arm for a shot.

"Rats," I say.

"Rats what?" she asks.

"Today's blood day. I forgot."

Every sixteen weeks since Duane died I go back to the hospital and donate blood. It makes me feel good, feel connected, and feel like somewhere somebody is getting some life from me at a time when he really needs it. Today's my day.

"Oh, right," Martha says.

"Blood day," Barry says, sipping his drink empty and refilling. "Sounds kinky. Let's do it."

Martha explains it to him.

"I'm in," Barry says, raising his glass.

"You can't go, and neither can I," she says. "They would never even use our blood, on account of the drinks."

"Even better. Less blood equals more buzz."

"Um, no," she says.

"Aw," Barry says. "Shame. We'll join you next time. Have fun, though. Bye."

I glare at him. Martha glares at me.

"Can I go with you?" Phil says, newly slathered and

sun-protected for probably a good fifteen minutes.

"How old are you, anyway?" I ask.

"Seventeen."

"Really? That means you can donate. You look younger, though."

"Everybody says that. My mom says it's because she only ever gives me organic beef. The regular kinds of beef have the steroids in them to help the cows grow faster, and then when people eat it, it makes them age quicker."

"I'm aging quicker just listening to you talk," Barry says.

Martha, crossing back to her chair, gives Barry a playful scolding slap on the arm.

It shoots through me like I've been Tasered.

What have they known each other for, a half hour? I'd kind of like my brother's widow to have a little more mourning stamina, frankly.

My blood is rising, so hot and so fast, I feel like I could shoot my deposit right from here and have it reach the hospital. That would be good. Then I could stay here and keep an eye on things.

"Please take that look off your face," Martha says to me. "It's making me nervous."

"And what happened to your eye?" Barry says, suddenly noticing.

"Can I use your bathroom before I go?" I ask her.

"Go," she says. I hop to my feet and move with a renewed sense of purpose toward the apartment building.

"Ow," Barry whines. "Jeezus, my eye."

"Eric," Martha shouts as I continue toward the bathroom. "Did you just elbow Barry?"

"No," I shout, not breaking stride. "I really have to go. Phil, I'll meet you out front."

"What is your *problem*?" she shouts.

I stare into the bathroom mirror. I hear Barry moaning through the small frosted louvered bathroom window. I hear Martha making a fuss over him and cussing me out.

"What is your problem?" I ask.

We buzz along the streets in the sunshine, and this feels like the best thing to be doing right now. A little ironic maybe, me and Phil tooling around town in an odd sort of a version of Martha and Duane's Rome fantasy, but it is making me feel better than I did back at Martha's. I'm relaxing gradually.

"I can't breathe," Phil says.

"What? What's the matter?"

"You're squeezing me really hard. I think I can hear my ribs cracking."

I did say it was gradual.

"Sorry," I say, and loosen my grip.

We park at the hospital, and I take Phil on a little tour without telling him it's a tour. I stand for ages in the grass, in the park, under the window of the room where my brother died. The split moss-green river rambles and chatters behind us, as it always does, while I stare up at the building. It's a beautiful place, really, a beautiful day.

And Phil might be the most patient person I have ever met.

I stop looking up for a minute, to look beside me. Without knowing exactly what my purpose is, he is standing almost shoulder to my shoulder, doing just what I am.

"Do you know what this is about?" I ask him.

"We're going to give blood, right?"

"Yeah," I say. "But this. This?" I gesture up at the window on the second floor.

He shrugs.

I grab him by the collar, whisper into his Duane ear. "You want to tell him, or you want me to do it?" I ask.

Phil chuckles at my silliness.

"Remember, Eric? He doesn't talk. He just hears."

I shake my head, at Phil's accumulating greatness.

"Right," I say solemnly. "Well, that room right there's where your ear bones came from."

He nods at me, turns, looks back up, and waves at the window.

We just then realize some old man in a gown is in that window, waving back at us. I get the creeps and pull Phil along to the hospital's main entrance.

Thirty minutes later Phil and I are lying side by side on beds in the blood donor area. We have small Band-Aids on our arms, and we are sipping orange juice and nibbling oatmeal-raisin cookies.

"Do you cry every time you give blood?" he asks.

"I told you, I was not crying! I have a very high threshold for pain. It's just sometimes the needle snags a nerve or some-thing, and that just makes your eyes well up."

"Right. I understand. But that's what crying is, isn't it?"

"Please just drink your juice. I am never bringing you here again."

It was not crying.

It was not pain.

And I do do it every time.

"Are you in love with Martha?" he asks me, with his juice straw still in his mouth. The nurse had to ask to see his driver's license three times before she believed he was seventeen, and if she saw him now with the straw, she would blow the blood right back into his arm and send him home.

"No," I say. "At least no more in love with her than the rest of the world. She and I, that way, would just be wrong."

"Not as wrong as her being with Barry, if you ask me."

"Oh," I say, gesturing so much that cookie crumbs are sailing around the room. "Oh, oh . . . Jeez, Phil, why do you have to say stuff like that? You can be a real wind-up, you know that?"

As demonstrative as I get, that's how reserved Phil remains. "You seem to get all . . . agitated, about Barry, and about Martha, and about—"

"Barry and Martha," I go off again.

"Yes."

"Well, I feel . . . a sense of responsibility. Duane's not here to handle things, and Martha shouldn't be stooping to—"

"Shhh," the nurse says, sticking her head around the corner. "Could you please hold it down? And try and relax, or you might get light-headed."

Too late.

Bing. I have a phone message. It's a photo of Martha, smiling radiantly. Sitting in that same chair in her backyard. She has put on a green straw floppy hat. Jeezus. She still has the green straw floppy hat that always made her look like she lived inside a permanent music festival. We have a photo somewhere of Duane in that hat. Jeezus.

And you can just about see a pair of feet in her lap. The photographer's feet.

Thanks, Barry. You're a sport, you really are.

"Okay, gentlemen. How are we feeling? Are we thinking it's about time to be up on our feet?"

I sit right up, swing my legs over the side of the bed. "Absolutely," I say.

It's a good thing she goes directly over to check on Phil, because my head becomes immediately swimmy. It's okay, though, because I've been through it before, and now it is just time to go. I want to be gone from here.

The rookie feels no ill effects.

"How long before I can come back and do it again?" Phil asks as the nurse leads him to the door with her hand sweetly on his back. He's that kind of guy, who inspires that kind of gesture.

"Four months," she says.

I follow along, feeling like *I* am the tagalong brother this time. And again, it's good that Phil is there and the nurse is there, keeping each other engaged, because something else is happening that happens every time I get to this point. I see the exit, I approach the exit, I feel the exit, and then it all floods me. The feelings come flooding, the good ones and the horrific ones and the soupy ones, and I don't know which way this is going to go, but I fight with my all to make sure it stays all inside, where it makes no mess.

And I think I'm winning, as I usually do, as I step through the doors into the sunshine with the flooding still flooding, bashing its way against my walls, trying to gush like my blood, our blood, out there now flowing whichever way toward whoever is gonna get it and wherever they're gonna take it.

I like helping the strangers by donating. But what I really come for are the floods.

PIECES

"The truth goes to the storyteller. And if you just keep talking, you'll eventually say everything."

MOTION

My parents are going away.

"What are you talking about?" I say, actually, rudely, awkwardly, and disgustingly laughing right at them. "You never go away."

"We are going on a retreat," Ma says.

"Is that a joke? How could you retreat any more than you already do? You only have the one gear, *reverse*. What's there left for you to retreat *from*?"

And in the most pointed articulation of the last decade, my parents stand there, looking at me, with eyes so sad they could drip like soft-boiled eggs right out of their heads, right along their bodies and onto the carpet on the floor between us.

"Don't do that," I say, actually raising a hand between my eyes and theirs.

"It's the church, Eric," Ma says.

"They run retreats like this," Dad says. "To help."

"To help people like us," she says.

Again, I'm touched, moved, dead impressed, and infuriated

by their melding into this single organism that they're becoming.

"Who are people like us, could you tell me? Not that I want to meet them, never mind live with them for a weekend. The last people I want to run into are people like us."

"You could come too, you know," Dad says.

"Should," Ma says. "*Should* come."

Again, boldly, triumphantly, mirthlessly, I laugh. Sonofabitch bastard, Eric, stop.

"Can I have my car keys back?" I ask once I have regained my composure.

I don't get the car keys back. But I do get the house.

They leave, for two days and two nights, to retreat and refresh and reboot whatever it is they want returned to them. I wish them luck. I really do. I hope that in the next forty-eight or so hours that church of theirs pays them back for all the time they've spent on their knees.

I'm alone.

Jesus Christ.

I'm alone.

It's not so funny now, is it?

Shut up. Not now.

If not now, when?

This doesn't happen, I realize. I don't live alone. I mean, I'm alone all the time, but I'm never left, completely, alone. Haven't been, since.

There's a song. I'm not much of a music guy, but there's a song. And there's a line in the song.

Leave
But don't leave *me*.

Chills.

Christ.

Here's a piece for ya, kid: If I don't want to stand out from the crowd, and I don't want to blend in with the crowd, what do I want?

Shut up.

For the twentieth time I watch the video the navy sent me about life in the service. For the twentieth time I stare at the impossible expanse of the blue, blue-green ocean, at the most opened-up world you will ever see. And for the twentieth time I cringe at the below decks, the steep steps between levels, the cramped tubelike corridors lined with piping and wiring and every other useful bit of kit strapped or bolted to the walls to maximize space and minimize air. There aren't doors between spaces; there are holes, really. The people aren't people; they are toothpaste, oozing from one area into another. The most closed little world you will ever see.

I start the film again, and the world opens up again and the battle begins again.

There was an aircraft carrier in port here four months ago. Open to the public for tours. I went. My goodness, what an awesome beast. And beautiful, the tower soaring, the radar gear spinning, clean lines and steel cables leading your eye to another perfect angle and another cold gray sculpture of military perfection. The jets, lined up at angles along either side of the ridiculous massive deck, still and silent but ready to jump. The great grotesque thing was everything I had ever dreamed it would be, overwhelming and efficient and deadly and frigid rigid.

And then below decks. An *aircraft carrier*, for Pete's sake.

As cramped as a rat hole. It was like, if the carrier was a sea eagle, then the below decks was a sea eagle killed and then pulled inside out.

I actually got sick. In the head. And it had nothing to do with the sea.

I play it for a third time. Loudly. There's that ocean.

I am alone. God, how did this happen?

"What are you doing?" I ask.

"Me? Really, me? What am I doing, right now, you mean?"

"Yes, Phil, that's what I mean. You and now and what?"

"Nothing. Just . . . nothing."

"Come on over."

Funny, ain't it.

Yes, it is. Very, very funny.

Shut *up*.

Funny, a phrase like "Come on over," which probably everybody says, probably all the time. I hear myself say it, and I have to wonder, have I ever said that, even once in my life?

My phone rings, and it is Melinda, as it has been several times in the last couple of days. Unlike those times, I answer.

"Well," she says, "this is a treat. Glad you decided to answer finally."

"Sorry. I've been busy. How are you? How is Dean?"

"We're both fine, thank you. Listen, I was just calling to say thanks."

"Thanks for what? I like parties. Thanks for having me."

"Well, you know, and for . . . helping me out."

"Helping . . . Oh, you mean the babysitting? So you could go on a date? With the guy who beat me up? Don't thank me. It was a pleasure. And educational for Dean, too, which is the important thing. I think every four-year-old should spend the evening of his birthday with a couple of people he had never met before. Otherwise, he'd probably just grow up to be strange with people."

There is a lot of dead air on the line. Normally I would consider that a victory.

"Talk, please," I say, like a more normal person.

"You're a pretty judgmental guy," she says softly.

"I guess that means one of us has judgment, anyway."

Dead air returns.

"What is your problem?" she asks.

Why does everyone have to keep asking that?

Well, not everyone. The doorbell rings.

"Come on up," I bellow in the direction of my bedroom window. "It's open."

"I guess you have company now," Melinda says, just a little bit forlorn.

"No," I say, "it's just Phil."

Phil walks through the door, may possibly hear that, gives me a sour look. "You know," he says, "the thing about those phones is that they go pretty much anywhere. So why are you all stuffed up here in your bedroom?"

"Say hello to sweet Phil for me."

"Hello, sweet Phil."

His face goes from sour to alarmed. "Are you drunk or something? I was thinking that might be why you called me, because I didn't totally understand. . . . If this is one of those booty-call things, I don't think I can—"

I am staring at him, and feeling the delight of grinning from ear to ear. He's like air-conditioning, this boy, soothing my fevered brow. I give him the *Calm down* wave, which seems to do for now.

"It can be lonely, you know," she says.

"What can?"

She sighs loudly. "Cruel, Eric? You didn't strike me as a cruel person."

I don't even want to sound like I'm sounding. Why am I sounding like I'm sounding?

"No, I never would, strike you. Bet Reg would, though, huh?"

And that appears to be the end of that conversation.

"Phil," I say, "do you like boats?"

"You're acting kinda weird," he says, but he puts up no struggle as I lead him down to the living room and the U.S. Navy's multimedia extravaganza.

My phone goes off again as the ship breaks the waves in the thrilling early going.

"You know," Melinda says, "I was only calling in the first place to say that we were thinking of coming down today, and maybe you might like to meet up for—"

"Have you considered Barry?" I ask.

"What?"

"Barry. As a cure for loneliness. I have a pretty strong hunch that if you hooked up with Barry, it might scratch an itch for both of you."

Once again it is me and Phil and a bunch of sailors.

It goes another five minutes before I have to respond to my phone. It doesn't ring or beep or anything this time. But it wants me.

"I am sorry."

That's the beauty of the text, I find. You can key in things you would never say, and it hardly hurts a bit.

As we buzz our way into town, I notice that Phil is getting the hang of imposing his will on city traffic. He is already a lot more assertive about weaving between and around cars, and seems actually to be enjoying it.

"You're a natural," I say into the steamy dry breeze.

"No, actually, I'm not," he says. "But I have to say, it feels a lot different doing this with you on the back than with my mom."

I shake my head behind his back. "Yeah, I'd say it would."

The city feels like it's in an upbeat mood, pedestrians in Red Sox attire all over the place indicating there is an afternoon game on. This is briefly a drawback as we run into thicker traffic snarls, but once we are through the dense part of the knot, we are whistling along by the river, the sailboats going both ways feeling like they are more our neighbors than the sooty smoggy vehicular traffic is. We have scheduled to meet up with Melinda and Dean but not for another half hour, so I aim my driver over across the bridge into Cambridge, where I am treating for an iced coffee.

We are sitting at a table on the sidewalk, sipping at two great big iced café mochas, and while Phil stares at every pretty passerby as if he's about to say "Take me to your leader," I am lavishing my attention on his scooter, parked at the curb ten feet away.

"You're a lucky man," I say to him, clinking glasses even though they're only clear plastic cups.

"Me? I am?" he says, and he's doing that boyish thing again, sipping at the straw and talking simultaneously.

I nod.

"Well, you know what? Right now I feel like I am. I don't think I've ever spent any time in Cambridge at all. And I really, really like it."

He makes me laugh. "You make me laugh, ya gimp."

He is draining the mocha, gurgly ice noises and all.

"That was a lot of coffee," I say, showing him my giant cup still half-full.

"Yes," he says, looking around, staring baldly at people as if he thinks he's invisible. "And it was a lot of fan*tas*tic coffee. And I never even drink coffee. I never go to Cambridge, and I never drink coffee, and look, I'm drinking coffee in Cambridge. On the *sidewalk*." He holds up his cup and waggles it around to get the last essence of caffeine to rise up to him. "We should get more," he says. I slide mine over to him. He takes it. I get more of a buzz when he revs up than when I do, so it's money well spent.

"I liked your navy movie," he says.

"Thanks. I didn't make it, though. The navy sent it to me."

"Why'd they do that?"

"Because I visited them, a recruiting visit."

"Yeah? You're gonna go? Into the navy?"

"Um. Yeah. I think so."

He has taken a break on taking in the sights for the moment, and now takes in the sight of me alone. He leans with some intensity toward me. "Why?"

"Why? What do you mean, why? Same reasons anybody goes into the navy. See the world. Learn something. Learn a skill or two. Learn about life. To experience the big wide world and especially the big wide beautiful ocean. A sense of purpose?"

The question inflection at the end of my sense of purpose would seem to contradict my sense of purpose a little bit.

Phil decides to notice something else. "I liked the ocean part, and the world part. Ship kind of looked like a floating jail, though."

"Well, it's not," I snap, because I don't know why it bothers me so much when people tell me what I am already thinking when I don't want to be thinking it, but it bothers me *so much.*

"Okay. Sorry. You would know better than me. When are you thinking of going?"

"This summer. Last summer."

"Next summer? Maybe then I'll go with you."

"Ah, Phil," I say, shaking my head. I feel like yelling at him, or at least talking him out of it, but I know there's no way they'd let him in anyway, with his bad ears and his mom clinging to his ankles.

"Ah, Eric," he says, smiley, reading probably something altogether different in me.

My phone bleeps. I look at it, expecting an update from Melinda.

It's Barry. I delete without reading, as that's an update I don't want.

I look back up at Phil enjoying every last milligram of that caffeine. He's sipping and grinning in all directions. He's waving. I look in the direction he's waving and see a trio of teenage girls waving back, and then I look back, expecting to see him blushing.

He isn't, though. Strike me blind if I'm wrong but I swear, since we sat down, I believe Phil's rice-paper complexion has acquired something you could call the beginnings of a tan.

This is it.

This is *it*, isn't it?

I grab Phil by the ear, by the Duane ear, and pull him almost roughly toward me. Phil laughs and plays along just fine.

I talk straight to the bones. "This is it, isn't it. This is your Rome. The sidewalk, the sunshine . . . the *life*. This is what you and Martha were talking about, about making it right here at home."

Phil waits for me to pause long enough, then turns to go nose to nose with me.

"*La Dolce Vita,*" he says with his sweet stupid smile.

"What?" I ask.

"*La Dolce Vita,*" he repeats.

"What does it mean?"

"I don't know."

"Where did you hear it?"

He shrugs. "I don't know. Someplace, I guess."

My phone rings, and this time it's Melinda.

"Where are you?" she says crisply.

"Cambridge. Where are you?"

"Outside the Children's Museum, just like I told you."

"You never told me—"

"Fine, I get it. You're still irritated and so you're going to play your sadistic games with me . . . *and* an innocent little boy. Bravo, Eric."

"No," I say, jumping to my feet, banging the metal mesh

table and knocking cups sideways. "No, no, no, not at all. I just misheard you, that's all. We are coming. Right now. Don't go away."

I wait for her response, tugging Phil by the shirt as I do, toward the scooter.

"Melinda? Hello, the silence thing can't accomplish much under the—"

"Fifteen minutes, Eric. It's already been a long drive, and it's a lot to ask a four-year-old in this heat, but because he is too young to know any better and has not yet developed great *judgment*, he is excited to see you and doesn't want to go in until you get here."

"On our way," I say, "on our way."

I'm strapping on my helmet with some urgency, while Phil appears to be posing for some kind of photo shoot for a lifestyle magazine, helmet under his arm, closed eyes up to the sunshine. I slap his face, sort of gently. I can hear his freckles erupting like popcorn across the bridge of his nose.

"Right, driver, to the Children's Museum."

"Excellent," he says. "I love it there."

"Of course you do."

The scooter sounds like a giant angry wasp as we zip right out into traffic, and Phil takes on all comers, all traffic, all elements. The sun is truly roasting now, and the helmet isn't helping.

What else is not helping is Phil's new caffeinated confidence.

"Hey!" I shout as he leans way hard into the turn that takes us onto the bridge back across the river.

"Hey," he shouts back in a much less serious tone.

He seems to have mastered the relationship between scooter and car, but scooter-truck, scooter-bicycle, scooter-pedestrian, scooter-dog, scooter-motorcycle, and scooter-scooter are all making this as complicated as the hardest computer game, and much more lethal. It's as if he's learning one element of road safety at a time, and that is good enough for him.

"Jeez!" I shout as we finally make it all the way across the bridge, only for him to pass a truck on the right and sideswipe a cyclist who hops the curb, screaming bloody revenge.

He giggles.

"Pull over, you!" I scream at him, like a cop, if the cop were on the back of your very vehicle.

"What?" he calls. "Here?"

"Right here!"

Displaying a charming alarming inclination to do whatever I say, Phil hooks left and pulls up onto the grass strip that leads right up to the brick bridge abutment.

"Somebody's a wicked backseat driver," he says when we have our helmets off our sweaty heads.

"What are you doing out there?" I shout.

"Getting somewhere!" he shouts back.

"That's just crazy stuff."

"I thought you would be impressed. I thought you would like that. It was fun, *and* efficient."

I can't believe my own eyes, but there it is, my finger in the air, waving vigorously in Phil's face.

"I realize what's so different with you on the back and not my mom. She's a lot more fun than you."

I will not be put off-message by that.

"Slow down. Arrive alive. Assertive, okay. Aggressive, not okay. Okay? You want to get yourself killed?"

The louder I shout, the more sweat I spray all over him, the more he appears to enjoy it.

"Whatever you say, Dad."

Dad? Me?

"Shut up."

"You know what might be cool? If you married my mom."

If I ever did have anything like mojo, it would appear to be well and truly dead and buried here on this grassy knoll of a traffic island.

I check my watch. "Dammit," I say. "We have to go. But get it under control. Less hurry, more speed."

He bounces onto the scooter seat. "Gee, I wait all this time for fatherly wisdom and it sounds just like fortune cookies."

I slap the side of his helmet far harder than any head-on collision is likely to do.

And still he is laughing into the teeth of everything as we jump back into traffic.

I know we are late already when we swing past the gigantic milk bottle outside the entrance on the wharf. It is a total carnival along the wharf, with umbrellaed picnic tables and people walking around with ice creams and tall drinks, and there can't be a more ideal summer spot anywhere in this city right now. There are loads of kids buzzing around, and I can't imagine what a hive it must be on the inside.

I direct Phil right around back, down an alley into a collection of converted warehouses that are now all residential.

I point him to a parking space right beside a Dumpster, as if I've lived here all my life.

"How do you know this is okay?" he says as we trot back around to the front of the museum.

"Look up there," I say, pointing at the perfect summer sky. "Then look back there," I say, pointing at the sharply rehabbed buildings.

"Okay?"

"Right. They're all at the baseball game. Trust me. As long as we get back before the end of the game, we're golden."

"Cool," he says. "How do you know all this stuff?"

I haven't been his dad long enough to tell him that I just make it up. So I run faster instead.

We get around front, around the milk bottle, where they are serving all that ice cream, through the tables and kiddies till we get to the ticket desk.

"Two, please," Phil chirps.

The woman behind the glass looks us up and down in a seriously dubious way. This causes me to look us up and down. We are both panting, sweating like a pair of plow horses. And Phil is so excited to get in and relive his childhood—which was still operational probably three months ago—that he is doing this odd stretch thing where he stands on tiptoe for three or four seconds, goes flat, up again on the toes, etc.

"Oh . . . no," I say. "We're meeting somebody. An actual kid. He's already here. With his mother, a woman."

I sound like I have a car waiting outside with a trunk full of hostages. And clueless Phil isn't helping either.

"Please, can we go in now?" he says anxiously, trading the toe-ups for a subtle running-in-place thing.

"Would you please . . . ," I say.

"Eric, man, I need a bathroom *right this minute*. I'm starting to realize there is a lot of stuff I need to learn about strong coffee."

"Pla-hah," I splutter out a laugh at his obvious internal chaos.

My laughter must have convinced the woman of something, because she takes our money—our whole lot of money, as it turns out—and we are in.

Phil dashes for the boys' room, and I tell him to come and find us when he is eventually finished.

"Or maybe you'll come and find me," he says as he disappears through the door.

When my phone call goes predictably unanswered, I go dashing through the place, working my way through one exhibit after another trying to find Melinda and Dean. There are *zones* of all kinds, building zones and climbing zones and science zones and several that should just be called *madness* zones that look like more fun than my whole childhood combined. There is an exhibit on the second floor that is all about caterpillars, and I have to confess that I have never given the caterpillar world nearly the credit it deserves for diversity, fun, and outright weirdness. There is one luminous green guy I watch munching a leaf for so long, ten full minutes pass before I realize it's all getting away from me. And even then I only break away because some Kobe-beef-fed seven-year-old future Dallas Cowboy crashes into me and snaps me out of it.

There is a whole exhibit on *The Wizard of* Oz. I have to resist the temptation to follow the yellow brick road, because once I scan and see that Melinda and Dean are not in there, the child me still wants to go in and get scared by the Wicked Witch of the West all over again, and throw apples at her. I have been aching to do that, for forever. The adult-ish me hauls me right out of there.

There are climbing walls stretching over two whole floors that look high enough to give me the dizzies, never mind kids, and I am scanning, scanning, scanning, suddenly all kinds of worried that Dean is up there, in jeopardy.

"What kind of a mother do you think I am?" Melinda says, right up close behind and making me jump.

I whip around. "The good kind, of course. Of course."

She has big rock-chick sunglasses on that force me to look at my reflection as she talks.

"Then, why were you so desperately looking for my little boy up on that wildly dangerous and inappropriate climbing structure when there is a far more age-appropriate one for him right over here?" She turns me a few degrees, in the direction of a more modest but still challenging wall, with slides for the tykes to come down once they have reached the summit. Dean is halfway up, and getting there like a spider monkey.

I turn back to her. "I wasn't looking for him up there. I was looking for you. So there."

"Hah," she says, looking again up at the challenging high wall.

There is a constant rain forest of sound in the place, and motion that makes the museum a thrill just standing there. Unless you're a kid, of course.

"Dean," Melinda calls as he heads right from the foot of the slide to the big kids' wall.

He's a good boy. He runs right over.

"Look who's here," Melinda says to him.

"Hi," Dean says, going shy behind his mother's hip.

"Did you go to the *Wizard of* Oz exhibit?" I ask.

"I love, love, love Professor Marvel's covered wagon," Melinda says.

"Flying monkeys made Mummy scream," Dean blurts.

"Eww," she says, waving her hands defensively in front of her. "They make my flesh crawl."

"Hah," I say.

"Hah, yourself," she says, pointing over my shoulder. "You better keep an eye on your little one."

"Hey, hey," Phil calls, hanging upside down from an elaborate rope climbing net, like the rigging on a tall ship but with little platform stages. I can already see the blood rushing to his face, his whole head a uniform orangey-red now.

"Get down here, will ya," I call to him.

Awkwardly he disentangles himself, nearly creates great comedy by sailing headlong to the platform below, catches, and rights himself.

"Look, Dean, the uncles have flown in," Melinda says.

Uncles. Who are these people? Who am I?

"Hey," Phil says, shaking Dean's hand. "I was like a human volcano downstairs, lemme tell you."

"Thanks for that," I say.

"Having fun, Dean?" Phil asks.

"I was trying to, but *she* stopped me."

"All right, all right, go on."

"Hi, Melinda," Phil says.

"Hello, Phil. Nice to see you again."

"I wanna go up there," Dean says, pointing to the ship's rigging where Phil just was.

"Oh, I don't know," Melinda says.

"I'll go with him," says Phil.

"Oh, good," I laugh. "That solves everything."

"I'll be good," Phil says, somehow managing to mock both himself and my skepticism.

"I know you will," Melinda says. "Off ya go, boys."

And off the boys go. Melinda and I take seats on a bench nearby.

"Really sunny outside, huh?" I say.

"Really sunny," she says.

"Not so sunny inside, though," I say. "What's with the shades?"

"Paparazzi issues," she says, nodding. She waves at Dean, who is halfway up the ropes. It's a long way up for his size, but Phil is right below him so he'll take the brunt of the impact when they both go down.

Not for the first time lately—not for the seventy-first time lately—the constituent parts of my brain are swimming in chaotic patterns around my throbby head, crashing into each other, repelling each other. I'm like a chameleon with the independently moving eyes. Only it's not just the visuals I am split-screening, but times, and people.

I cannot take my eye off Melinda and the glasses.

I cannot take my eye off her boy, and my boy.

"We came here."

"What?" she says, sounding as swimmy as me.

"Duane and me. We came here, did this stuff. Cripes." It is rushing back now, seizing me. "A million years ago. It was one of the things we did. Parents were into this stuff, the science museum, natural history museum at Harvard, aquarium.

Not all interactive like a lot of parents, or like him." I gesture toward Phil, scrambling down the net to retrieve his shoe, which was pulled off by one eight-year-old and thrown down to another one on the ground. Dean, laughing wildly, is climbing down even faster to help. "There was one exhibit, Duane stuck my head in a wooden vise, and then left to go see something else. Eventually somebody else's father came to release me when his own kids were laughing so hard that they couldn't help. My own parents didn't even believe me when I tried to tell them.

"But anything they could bring us to, and just *be* there with us, was good. And it *was* good. Duane and me, we didn't need a lot, aside from each other.

"I think, anyway. That's how I felt, anyway."

I turn both of my eyes to her. "I think, after all, they might have been good parents. In there somewhere," I tell her. I finally, finally tell.

"I think, undoubtedly, they were," she says.

I reach out, slowly moving my hand to her face.

"Don't, Eric," she says, but does not raise a hand to my hand, does not pull her face from my hand.

I raise the sunglasses off her face, just enough.

I breathe deeply three, four, five times before I can speak. "The work of a left-hander," I say.

The lid of her right eye is that purple-meets-green awful color that should not exist anywhere. The eye bones are raised swollen, not unlike the one he gave me.

I lower the sunglasses back over her eyes.

"Don't say anything," she says.

"No, of course not," I say. "Did you tell anybody about this?"

"That's not not saying anything, Eric. That's saying something."

"It's not saying; it's asking. Did you tell anybody?"

"That's what I'm doing now. Right?"

Our boys fly right past us, toward something called Johnny's Workbench. "We'll catch up," she calls after them, though nobody asked.

"Yeah, but I'm not a cop, am I?"

"No. You're . . . a friend. You're . . . a brother. You're . . . something."

Something. Something. That might be the best one yet.

"Is that why you're here today? Is that why you came to town? You running away?"

She gives it all body language, the eyes well hidden. She shrugs, she nods, she gives me upturned palms, she shakes her head, she shrugs again.

"Okay," I say, because, well, I got nothing else but "okay." I hope "okay" is okay for now.

I take Melinda by the hand, and she lets me. I lead her toward the boys, toward Johnny's Workbench and KidStage and Science Playground and the Recycle Shop, where we will wallow in some childhood.

PIECES

"The only time a strong person loses is when he turns on himself. He can't win that one. Other than that, he's indestructible."

SERIOUS CHAP

"His last name is Crocket, right?" Melinda says out of the corner of her mouth, spylike. "But he pronounces it like the game, Croquet. Crow-Kay. That's what kind of a jackass he is."

"Ha," I laugh, bringing around the milk for Dean's second bowl of Cap'n Crunch. "Duane used to feel like that about people who pronounced both of the Ds in Wednesday. Couldn't stand them."

Melinda is wearing her sunglasses at the breakfast table. She and Dean spent the night in Duane's old bedroom, which *still* has the old Lord of the Rings–themed furnishings, which he insisted on keeping way past when he had a kidlike attachment to them and had moved into the irony zone. No way anybody's changing them now.

"Do you really need those?" I say, nodding at the glasses. "Here?"

She looks over toward Dean, who is munchin' the Crunch and flipping through one of my brother's comics, one in an extensive collection. Hellboy. Happy boy.

"Yes," she says.

"No," I say. "I mean, fine, it's your face, so whatever. I just mean, no, it's not *necessary* at this point in place and time."

Melinda picks at her scrambled eggs. Leaves the glasses on. I am not a very good cook. I do passable scrambled eggs. I feel unbelievably in love with her at this moment. The eggs have little shreddings of ham laced through.

Without looking up she removes the glasses. My heart jumps. What a noodle I am.

"You don't like my eggs," I say.

"I'm a vegetarian," she says, picking the ham bits out, setting them aside, then leaving both segments of food uneaten.

"Rats," I say. "I'm sorry. I should have asked. That was . . . Wait a minute. You ate pizza at Chuck E. Cheese."

"I don't eat pork products."

"Oh, okay, how 'bout I . . . Hey. You ate pepperoni *and* sausage pizza."

"Right," she says solemnly, nodding, nodding. She turns her eyes up to me. "Your scrambled eggs are watery."

"Arrggh," I say, snagging the plate from her as she giggles. "You could have just told me."

"I was afraid you might kill yourself."

"Oh, come on. I'm not like that."

"The eggs seemed very important to you. And you are a very serious chap."

"What? I'm a lot of fun."

My phone blips. Barry.

"Away, jerkwad," I snap while sending his text unread on an untethered walk into cyberspace.

"Well, that was fun," Melinda says.

"Oh, that was Barry."

She laughs. Even her green-purple eye crinkles attractively. "Maybe you are a little overly critical on that score?"

"Um, no," I say. "I am accurately well-judged critical on that score."

"He is a little coarse, I'll grant you. But he seems harmless enough."

"Oh, really? You know what he's been harmlessly up to for the last two days?"

"Ooohhh, gossip," she says, leaning up closer across the table. "What's he been up to the last two days?"

I begin shoveling Melinda's uneaten food into my mouth, way too fast, like you do when you are too wound up really to be eating.

And when you find yourself in the middle of saying something stupid.

"Ah, well, I don't strictly know."

"Gee, that sounds criminal," she says.

"But he keeps trying to text me the details, and that's how I know it's gotta be creepy."

"What you call creepy, somebody else might call a laugh."

"What? Oh, so he's fun and I'm not, is that it?"

She pauses, but it is simply for effect. "Yeah, that's probably it."

"This is outrageous," I say.

"Listen, I didn't say he is a better guy than you are, because he most certainly is not. But while you have some fine qualities . . ."

"I am fun," I protest, mirthlessly.

"More, please?" Dean says, waving around a completely licked-clean bowl.

"Sure," I say, jumping up. As if this will establish my fun credentials.

"Surely *not*," she says, taking the bowl from the boy. "Do you not have any idea how these things"—she's gesturing at her son—"work?"

"Yeah," I say. "Ya feed 'em, then watch 'em go."

"Uh-huh. Right. Dean, you can go back into Duane's room, look at some more comics if you like. But no more Cap'n Crunch now."

"You can have an apple," I say.

He practically leaves a vapor trail, running in the direction of the comics, away from the apple.

"So, how *is* the lovely Martha," Melinda says.

I take the cereal bowl from her, along with the now also licked-clean egg plate. I am washing them at the sink.

"Who mentioned her?" I say. I sound twelve.

"You did. Not in so many words . . ."

"I don't exactly know, if you must know. I haven't talked to her in . . ."

"A couple of days?" she says.

I think I am growling a little into the sink as I wash out Dean's orange juice glass. But at the same time, the old conflicted stuff flicks up.

I am liking the domestic thing. I am liking doing things for somebody else. For these bodies else.

Melinda comes over and hops up onto the counter a few feet away. She sits and chats while I wash.

"Barry and Martha, huh?"

"How old are you?" I splurt.

I wince at myself, take two handfuls of washing water and splash-attack my face to wash as much of the idiot off as I can.

"I'm twenty-six," she says. "Twenty-six hard ones, though."

Don't ask me how old I am, Melinda.

"How old are you?"

My voice is going to crack. It is. The thing is gonna crack, is in fact silently cracking right this second, and so I cannot participate in this perfectly normal and friendly and warm *adult* conversation because of it. So, I take adversity and make fun from it.

I turn in her direction and hold up six dripping fingers. Once, twice, thrice. Eighteen. How cleverly done.

See, I am fun.

"I thought you were older," she says.

Cracking isn't a remotely suitable word for what my voice is doing inside me right now. She has to think I am some kind of simp or totally deviate or something. I continue washing the egg dish as if it has been very bad and needs spiritual cleansing, and I look, again and again in Melinda's direction with a smile that is aching to be charming but almost certainly looks like I need to take a dump.

My phone rings now. A call, not a text. The phone, ringing and vibrating uncontrollably much like its owner right now, is on the counter between us. I am acting like it's not there.

"You not going to get that?" Melinda asks.

I make a mumbling noise that doesn't even have meaning to me.

Melinda picks up the phone and looks at the screen.

"It's Martha," she says.

I make the incomprehensible mumbling sound, but louder, and deeper down into the sink.

"Can I answer it?" she says.

My face whips in her direction. I give her the toilet-face smile. She takes that as a yes.

Arggh.

Melinda takes my phone, and Martha, off into the living room.

"Helloooo," Melinda says in a far too suggestive and loaded tone of voice.

•So finally at least I can stop washing the stupid dishes. I dry my hands and hop up onto the counter where Melinda just was. It is the ideal vantage point to take in the view of this life in this house.

I am aware of how frequently Duane would take this exact position in this exact spot, for the purpose of observing, commentating, mortifying, and of course philosophizing.

"If there is one thing I know in this world, then this is the thing I know . . . ," I say to the house and its inhabitants past, present, and future.

"What are you doing, Uncle Eric?"

The first thing I'm doing is practically peeing the kitchen counter with fright at the shock appearance of the four-year-old witnessing me pretending to be my dead-but-still-more-fun-than-me brother.

The second thing I am doing is balancing myself against toppling right over off the counter at the sound of that phrase, title, whatever we might call it.

Uncle. Eric.

What a doink I am, to get so excited over that. Doink.

I hop off the counter under my own power and walk up to the boy, who is holding another publication in his hand, but it is not a comic book. Not technically, that is.

"Whatcha got?" I ask.

He extends the magazine. "Will you read this to me?"

It's the elaborate, bright, and breathtaking brochure the United States Navy sent me. It is a handsome thing, no matter what one's opinion of the armed services.

"Where'd you get this?" I ask him, flipping through the pages with renewed admiration. Same as happens every time.

"It was in my room. On the floor next to the bed."

Honestly. How many times can I be split right down the middle, like a firewood log struck perfectly with the axe, like the river running both ways beside the hospital?

"My room." There is a beautiful and well-mannered little boy talking about that room, *that room, right there, into that corridor and then left*, as *his* room, which was "my room" to some other boy before.

And then there's *my* navy literature, turning up in that room. When, I could swear, I have not been in that room in a year, other than to show those two to it last night.

I could swear.

I could swear.

"It's not so much a reading book, Dean," I say.

Nevertheless, we head for the couch. As we enter the living room, Melinda, deep in an alarmingly serious conversation with Martha, gets up and walks out. I put that situation out of my mind and I work up a narrative about the navy, the ships in the pictures, the ports of call, the call of duty, the duty of citizenship.

I like the sound of me there. I like the sound of me talking to the boy.

And I think I might make a good recruiter.

"Are you gonna be in the navy?" he asks. He is leaning right into me, the length of his little warm frame lined right up alongside me. This is probably the longest sustained physical contact I have had with another person since I was his age. I don't even want to flee. "Are you gonna be on that boat there? Or that one?" He's pointing first at a nuclear submarine that can stay underwater for months at a time, then at an aircraft carrier.

"Yes, I think I probably am gonna be in the navy." Then I point at the same pictures. "The sub, not if I can help it. The carrier, maybe."

"I'm gonna join the navy too," he says.

I laugh, so I can at least pretend not to be as stupidly proud as I am. "What about your dog? They won't let you take your dog into the navy with you. Where is he, anyway?"

"Daddy says Skye was his dog. Skye's gone with Daddy."

"Skye's gone with Daddy?" I say matter-of-factly.

"I wish Daddy was gone to the sky," is what I'd rather say.

Melinda comes in, carrying the phone without talking on it. Her nose is red, her face dewy with tears. "That poor, wonderful girl," she says, handing me the phone.

Naturally, I get furious.

"Barry. Is it Barry? I *knew* that situation was nothing but bad news. I'm gonna go over there now and break every single—"

"Oh, it has nothing to do with Barry, ya macho maniac. It's Duane."

"We're joining the navy," Dean says.

"I am not a maniac," I say. "I'm a concerned citizen."

"The navy, eh," she says.

Melinda plunks herself down on the couch on the other side of me from Dean. It's a me sandwich, and the sensory effect is nearly overwhelming. Like I could get a really sweet nervous breakdown from it.

"So, what are we doing today?" Dean asks cheerily.

"Um," Melinda says softly, glumly, and I worry she may suggest going home or something equally foolish.

"You don't have to go?" I say.

She sighs. "As of tomorrow I will have officially used all of this year's sick time." She shifts to mock euphoria. "So as of today, we're great!"

"Then, I have an excellent idea," I say.

"Did your parents used to bring you here as well?" she asks as we board the beautiful beast.

"No, not this one. This was school-trip stuff. Three times, in fact, and for some reason, Duane's classes never did it. He would always wave it in my face that his class was going to Canobie Lake Park or something and we were stuck with sad Old Ironsides. I'm pretty sure that was the reason he never got the naval thing at all but I did."

"I can see it," she says, looking up at the endlessness of the mast shooting the sky, "and I'm not even a little boy . . . like you two."

She looks down from that sky view to take in the sight of Dean and me practically fondling one of the frigate's forty-four cannons. I feel it, all over again, like I felt it the first time and then again and again. This is the very definition of awe-inspiring.

But more. There is way more now.

Dean has both hands on the lacquer-black cannon, and he is tracing every curve, every bump on the old iron gun as if he were a blind person working it out. We pass each other as we are doing essentially the same thing, working our way around the cannon, from the barrel to the breech and up the other side again. I am getting a new thrill that has never been part of it before.

I am sharing the awe, and watching it take root.

"Stand there, you two," Melinda says when we are at the breech.

We stand, on either side of the cannon, each with a hand on it, posing for her. She raises her phone, and freezes us there forever.

"Pretty great, huh?" I say to Dean as he scoots from the cannon, across the polished wooden deck to the ship's wheel.

"Pretty great, huh," he yelps.

I am caught up in it now. I run, following Dean everywhere. I have never seen such rope work. I realize this rigging has been more or less in place since 1797, but it still shocks me whenever I see it. It's about a zillion miles of rope, but none of it is confused or confusing. All has an obvious sense of purpose and design even if it would take me a couple of lifetimes to figure it out.

"Can we go downstairs?" Dean asks.

"'Below decks,'" I correct, sounding like a dinko boat bore. "And yes."

Just then, as an old man and woman head down the

gangway off the ship, a sailor blows a whistle and salutes and announces to the crowd, "Captain Winston Broad, United States Navy, retired, disembarking."

There are scores of tourists milling around, and probably three quarters of them salute. Including me. Including, after me, Dean.

That is respect. That is something special. That is the United States Navy, is what I'm thinking.

We follow along with a group headed for the steps to the below decks. Dean has to touch everything as we pass, and so do I. Melinda, being less boyish and susceptible to the foolishness of giant toys and things that go *boom*, is all the same totally impressed with the historic structure we are privileged to be on. The beams, the curvature of the wooden deck that allows the water to run off the sides, the zillions of rivets making the old sides as iron as iron, all prompt comment from her.

"I might not know warfare, but I know beauty," she says as we descend, "and this is high art."

I feel a second wave of rush, of pride, of success. You would think I owned this old boat, and that I built it myself. But honestly, this is going as perfectly as it could, with me and Dean and the USS *Constitution* all clicking in that way boys and boats do, and me and Melinda and the USS *Constitution* clicking in that other way, the way of serious, adult people who appreciate greatness and beauty and history however we find it.

I am in love, with this ship. Pretty fond of the navy right now too.

We visit the sick bay, the surgeon's cockpit, the sail loft, and the gun decks. There isn't much about the tour that isn't fascinating. The captain's cabin might be the world's greatest hotel room, with windows right over the water and its own two cannons. The beds are a little bit small, and the sight of the hacksaw in the surgeon's tool kit is a little unnerving, but mostly the truth is that this setup looks more comfortable, roomy, and even romantic than anything I have seen on any of the modern vessels.

"I am joining this navy," Dean shouts as we emerge again onto the top deck and into the hazy sunshine. Thinking each vessel is a navy.

There must have been something special about the last gent we heard piped off the ship, because, while we didn't hear the words, his departure is followed by the shock surprise of a rocking one-gun salute, which pops my ears and my heart, waking up the primal me. It also sets off a couple of car alarms and causes Dean to shout even louder, "I am joining this navy."

"Me too," I say.

"Me too," Melinda says.

"Mom," Dean says, mortified. "Navy's not for moms."

As unenlightened as he may be there, I choose to believe he just means not for *his* mom. So I leave it. I am a chicken, really, and selfish, and what I really want is to preserve this solidarity moment between the boys for as long as I can.

And also, I wonder for a minute which one of us is recruiting the other.

This navy. He's got a good point. If my ten-year-old heart in my eighteen-year-old body could find itself in *this* navy, I'd be gone already. I would.

We are standing outside the USS Constitution Museum, where I did, yes, buy the boy a small ship replica and a history picture book about Old Ironsides. He can't stop turning the model around and around in his hands, checking all the angles against the big reality we just left.

"You didn't have to do that, you know," Melinda says.

"Yes, I did," I say emphatically.

She sighs, charmingly. "Yes, I suppose you did."

"So, where will we go now?" I say, beating Dean to the punch because I am still more boy than he is. I scan around the Charlestown Navy Yard, where the condominiums ring us but the working waterfront still has commercial ships and coast guard vessels and one modern navy warship berthed right in front of us. The world seems big and accessible at the same time right now.

I finally look away from the port, to the lady, and she is looking at her feet, then up at the sky.

"What?" I ask.

"Home," she says, nodding a bit sadly, a bit sheepishly. "Home, Eric, is where we need to go now."

"What?" I say. "No. Come on. . . . It's too soon yet. You only just—"

"It's time. I can't thank you enough—"

"Yes, you can," I say. "Sure you can." My voice is a bit desperate, like a kid. And at the same time entirely unlike a kid. I'm not even certain what I mean by what I'm saying, but it isn't slowing me down at all from saying it. "Thank me, Melinda. Thank me enough. Thank me too much, even. I mean, there's no need to thank me, of course, for anything, so let me get that right out of the way first. I have had the most awesome time. So I should be thanking you. But . . . Yeah, I should be thanking you. Let me. Give me a chance. . . . Stay."

She comes right up to me, holds my face in the most wonderful way a face can be held. She takes one flat palm and presses it to my cheek, then holds her own cheek against my other cheek.

"You are extraordinary. You are wonderful. You are a wonderful friend. And Dean and I have to return to our real, messy, imperfect lives now. You can't just provide some ideal, uncomplicated fairyland for us."

"Yes, I can," I say, without having any notion of how I could. "I can. I can do exactly that for you."

"I'll call you," she says.

"You can't go," I say. "You don't even have your stuff. Your bag is still back at the house."

She shakes her head.

"You packed it already," I say. "Before we even left. It's in the trunk, yeah?"

If the rush of thrill that came with the cannon explosion has an opposite sensation, my stomach is feeling it right now. I look at Dean, who is sitting on the ground, balancing the open book on one knee while trying to match the model ship up to one of the illustrations on the high seas.

"We could give you a lift back home," she says.

I shake my head. "I'll make my way. It's a lot easier for you to get onto I-93 from here, rather than going all the way back up through town and down again."

"I will call you," she says, pulling Dean by the hand up off the ground.

"I believe you," I say.

"Dean, are you going to say good-bye to Uncle Eric, and thank him for everything?"

He looks up from his book, which is flopping around in his non-boat hand. "Why? Where's he going? Where are you going?"

"I'm going home," I say. "And so are you."

"My home? I don't want to go to my home," he says.

"We need to, Son," she says. "Daddy's wondering where you are. And you want to see Skye, don't you? Skye misses you."

"Nhhh," he says, then looks up at me for the first time, really, since he became a boat owner.

"Good-bye, Uncle Eric," he says.

"And . . . ," Melinda says.

He pauses. "Good-bye and good luck," he says.

I laugh.

"Sorry," she says. "One of his TV characters says that all the time. Dean, thank Eric."

"Thank you," he says, his attention already recaptured by the magnetism of the model ship. As it should be.

I offer him my hand. "See ya," I say.

He shifts the book to under his left arm. He shakes my hand.

"I'll call you," Melinda says as she turns toward the parking lot and her crappy car and crappy New Hampshire and the crappy people who live there.

"I know," I say, and watch them walk for about ten feet before I turn a nice sharp military turn and march briskly in the opposite direction.

PIECES

"Love is what it's all about. If you see it coming, duck. If you don't see it coming, you're boned."

THE SWEET LIFE

I'm alone again. It's like the house gets a little bit bigger every time I come back to it now.

I need to run.

Since I quit playing organized sports a few years ago, I haven't exercised with the same regularity, or ferocity, as before. But then, in the past year or so, I have found myself taking more frequent runs again, and more lengthy ones. If I am going into the service, I have to show up with a certain level of fitness or pay a serious price for my laziness. That's what got me back to it.

And one other thing really got me back.

All I wanted to do after Duane died was go physically crazy. I wanted to smash things up, I wanted to get into fights, I wanted to run things over with the car. I sincerely, passionately wanted to do these things.

I knew, however, that this was probably wrong.

But so what? Who cares what you know, when you *feel?* Feel trumps think, in my experience, every time.

Lucky for me, and for the world, old impulses kicked in, and when the angry energy got too irresistible, I got out on the road.

The first run after the long layoff was almost comical. As if I had never been down this road before, I skipped the stretching, skipped any kind of warm-up, skipped the slow steady gradual increase of pace. I barreled, showing that road who was boss.

I really showed it at about the one-mile mark, when I veered right off the road, down into a ditch by a tree by the parkway, and barfed up a good three days' worth of meals and bile and anger.

I daresay I am more sensible these days. And more fit.

I had missed my runs.

So I run my run now, and the *thump-thump-thump* of it is the most cooling and soothing thing I have felt in days. The urge to choke, to mist up, even—which I have felt since watching Melinda and Dean walk away and which I would still never admit to them or anyone else—is being crunched, trampled under my feet.

Thump-thump-thump-thump, I pass the river, which leads down that way to the hospital, where I will not be going. I head around the pond, up the back roads, through the perfect steamy dry hot quiet of a dead summer Saturday. I go up hills, through neighborhoods, down hills again. I veer almost to the cemetery, which was once upon another lifetime an absolute must on my running days and most other days but won't be part of anything today.

I run, and I run and I run, forgetting the empty house that is behind me and ahead of me, forgetting the beautiful fools of New Hampshire, forgetting Duane and my parents and retreats of any kind, forgetting psycho jerk Barry and especially Martha, crying Martha.

I feel my left hamstring start to grab. Then more, then more, like a steel cable being mechanically stretched, tightened, pulled. This shouldn't be. This means I did lose control, I did exceed speed, because if I am not sprinting, my hamstring is not biting, and holy mother, is it biting me now.

I slow down, slow down. I have to stop. I stretch, stretch it out. That kills me, but I have to do it. No, I don't. I have to stop. I am on the return run, probably three miles from home. After a few minutes of walking, it feels better. It is calm, and loose, and I begin a light jog again.

Holy smokes! I might have torn the thing, and just thinking about tearing that particular muscle, big hard thick cable-y thing that it is, makes me shudder. Makes me shake, and shudder and sink right down to the curb, and hold my head in my hands, makes me choke and mist up. This, dammit, hurts. It hurts.

I am sitting on the curb, head-in-hands humiliation washing right down me with the sweat and what all, and I think I could just possibly stay right here, calcified forever, a piece of curb, left undisturbed, in the silent summer swelter.

Until I hear in the distance. Sounds like a cicada. Possibly a swarm of hornets. Possibly one of those remote control airplanes that run on gasoline.

But as it gets closer, it is clearly none of those things, and I have to look up. To see the vision. It's Phil, on his scooter, zooming right down on my position. I watch him grow bigger and bigger in my vision, until he is right here, in person, in color.

"What are you doing here?" he says.

"What are you doing here?" I say.

"I asked first."

"I'm running," I say. "Can't you see?"

"How come running looks so much like crying?"

I jump to my feet and start marching down the street.

That is a lie, of course. Because, while I do get up somewhat quickly, and I do create some down-street motion, I am doing no marching. I barely manage not to howl, as the hamstring now feels not only like somebody has torn it roughly in half, but that someone has also set the two loose ends on fire.

"I'll tell you how come it looks so much like crying," I say through gritted teeth. "*Shut up*, that's how come."

"Oh," he says.

"And I asked you what you are doing here."

"Right. Well, I was on my way to your house, funny enough. You want a ride, or will I just meet you there?"

"I don't recall inviting you over, *Philip*."

I am pretty well dragging my leg behind me now. In the deserted street, with Phil following close behind me while pretty much walking the scooter, we look like a reverse zombie flick where the creatures are hunted by the nerds.

"You didn't invite me. But I called your phone. And when you didn't answer any of the times—"

"How many times, Phil?"

"Six. And when you didn't answer, I thought I would come by. You know, to check on you. 'Cause of how scared you are to be alone and—"

"I'm not scared. Shut up. You don't know anything about me. What's with everybody thinking they know me all of a sudden? Don't know me, okay? I'd just as soon not be known, so just, don't."

He sort of foot pedals along for a few more yards before speaking again. But it turns out to be worth the wait.

"My ears were burning," he says.

"Uh, excuse me?"

"That's what I should have said. When you asked me what I was doing here. I should have said, 'My ears were burning and that's why I came.' 'Cause I sensed you needed me. Or, maybe ear. My *ear* is burning. Get it?"

"I get it." I am actually more impressed and amused than I am letting on. "Dork."

"Yeah, that would have worked out better than the answer I did give you, which really didn't work out very well at all."

"Not really, no."

"So, are you gonna be smart and take a ride, or will I just leave you here limping and crying in the street?"

"*You* are gonna be limping and crying if—"

He revs his little engine to shut me up. And it works.

How did this guy get so confident all of a sudden?

Phil keeps himself amused watching my navy video over and over while I take a hot recuperative bath. I am not entirely recuperated by the time I emerge into the living room. Phil is concerned for my well-being.

"Are you gonna go to the doctor?"

"Why would I do that?"

"Because one of your legs doesn't appear to work at all."

"It's fine," I say. "A little rest is all I need."

"Whatever you say. But don't think I'm always gonna be there whenever you're stranded."

"No, I wouldn't—"

"Actually, I probably will," he says, grinning up madly at me.

"Thanks," I say, instead of telling him what a sad, lame little man he is.

Or how pleased I am at what a sad, lame little man he is.

"Your phone's been doing stuff," he says, gesturing at it on the coffee table.

I check. I have texts, from Barry, of course. And I have three missed calls, all from Martha.

I have to call her. I can't not call her.

"Hey," I say.

"Hey," she says. "Where you been?"

"I do bathe occasionally."

"Okay, I approve. Listen, we've been trying to get ahold of you for ages. We want to see you."

We.

"We? 'We,' Martha? Are we a 'we' now? Do you have to say 'we'?"

She waits me out.

"Are you all right, Eric? Because frankly you sound mental. You got a phobia about the word 'we' now, on top of all your other weirdnesses?"

I wait her out.

"Fine," she says, "we are not a 'we.' But I'll tell you what, Barry is not the goblin you made him out to be. Not by a long shot."

"Yeah," I hear shouted in the background.

"Ah, Christ, Martha."

"Just stop it, ya big baby, and grow up. Really, it's time. For everybody."

I would like to know what she means by that. I won't be asking her, though.

"What did you call for?" I ask instead.

"I want to talk. I want to come over. Can I come over? I'll bring Chinese food."

"You'll bring Chinese, and Barry, yeah?"

"Yeah. Yeah, that's part of it. I think . . . you should give him a chance. I think it would be good. For you."

If I tell her how much I hate this right now, it could only make things look worse. I could only be a bigger baby, a weirder weirdo, if I put up any fuss.

"Sure, let's make a party of it. But bring enough food. Phil's here too."

"Is he? Excellent. That's excellent. He's good for you too, you know that? Hi, Phil."

"Martha says hi, Phil."

"Hi, Martha. A party, cool."

I am getting more depressed by the minute.

"Dude."

"Hi, Barry," I say as he walks in and past me carrying bags of aromatic Chinese food. But almost instantly he washes from my mind as I see Martha. And the suitcase.

I brighten right up. "You're staying over? Here?" I say, excited like a kid, grabbing her bag like a proper man. "I'll set you up in Duane's room, yeah? Jeez, this is a lot of stuff for one night," I say.

"That's because it's for a lot of nights," she says. "It's for *all* the nights."

Now I am really confused. Excitement being quickly overtaken by apprehension.

"Okay," I say uncertainly, "but I think my parents might take some convincing."

She squeezes my arm and pushes me into the house, into the kitchen.

Barry and Phil are assigned to get us all set up for eating around the coffee table in the living room, while Martha fills me in.

"I'm going, Eric. I have to. It's been so hard here. Harder than I even thought it was gonna be. Harder, even—a little harder every day."

Barry comes in, grabs a roll of paper towels, scoots out again.

"That's because of him, I'm sure," I say.

"No, it isn't. Will you stop? Barry has been great. He's been wonderful to talk to, and you know, if you actually give him a chance . . . Come on. Have you not recognized a certain panache there?"

"No," I snap. "I don't recognize anything like it."

"Open up," she says, knocking on my forehead like a door.

"No," I say, just to be petulant.

Martha leads me by the hand toward the living room and the food and the guys. I stare at her hand the whole way, feel all of its warmth, squeeze it just a little too hard, but she allows it.

"You're joining the navy?" Barry says as the video winds down one more time.

"Yes," I say.

"Aw, don't," he says. I wait for the punch line, but he appears to be finished.

"Stay," Phil says, and there is obviously no punch line on the horizon.

"Barry is taking over the lease on my apartment," Martha says.

Barry is grinning away, and clapping two curried wontons together like one of those windup monkeys playing the cymbals. "My father has agreed to co-sign for me," he says. "And to pay the first four months' rent. And move all my stuff out of his basement himself. And change all the locks at his place, which is a little mean-spirited, don't you think?"

"Where are you going?" I ask Martha.

She smiles shyly. "Rome. Rome was supposed to be here, remember? That's what I came back for. Only to find it gone. I have to find Rome, Eric. And I just figured, I might as well start in Rome."

I'm not sure what prompts me at this moment, but I get out my phone and show Martha the photo that Melinda sent me earlier of me and Dean on the ship.

"My God, that is so sweet," she says, then passes it around to the other guys.

"Awesome," says Phil.

"You know," Barry says, "I've been thinking about that Melinda—"

"Oh, God, Barry, no," I say, shoving boneless spare ribs at him as if they are the solution here. "Please, don't do that."

Barry laughs hard at that. "Fine," he says. "Nobody ever said I'm not a gent." Then he turns to Phil. "So, Phil, what's *your* mother look like? Got any photos on ya?"

Phil recoils silently, deeply back into the couch cushions, hiding behind a jumbo fried shrimp.

We talk for ages over the Chinese food and a two-liter Sprite and a jug of sangria that tastes like Hawaiian Punch.

I must have said too much about the trips to the Children's Museum and Old Ironsides, because at some point both Barry and Phil start referring to me as "Dad."

"Excuse me, boys," Martha says, and heads off to the bathroom.

"Jeez, I thought she'd never go," Barry says. "The girl's like a camel. So right, the thing I was thinking about Melinda was . . ."

"Oh, God," I groan.

He doesn't even break stride. "I mean, it's kind of strange, right? How my liver and her kidney used to live together, all wrapped up inside your brother, right? What does that make me and her? Do I have to take that into consideration? I keep having this thought, like what if I bump into something up inside there that was once part of Duane and now Duane's part of me . . . Is that too weird . . . ? And this guy's got the ear bones, which were right next to the brain, so, like, does all this stuff we do echo in his head too? Wait, be cool."

Martha comes back into the room, stands in the doorway taking the scene in.

"Right," she says. "It's silent in here. Eric's eyes are bloodshot and bulging. Phil looks like he's just been scared straight in prison. I'm guessing Barry's been talking."

"Excellent," he says, with a triumphant double fist pump.

She continues to stand, however, which doesn't feel good. She checks her watch, which feels worse.

"I have to go," she says.

I look up at her from my spot on the floor. I immediately flash back to the first time I saw her, probably from pretty much this same angle, this same spot, when Duane first brought her home and I first fell into that crush.

"Stay," I say.

She smiles generously, finally. "No, Eric."

I stand, walk right up to her, getting my face in her face, knowing it will never be there again.

"I have a cheap flight out of Newark," she says with her eyes closed. "With about fourteen stopovers along the way. Want to take me to the bus station?"

I nod, my head against her head.

"We'll all go," Barry says, jumping to his feet.

I grab him firmly by the shoulders. I stare hard at him, into him, like I haven't since about ten minutes after we met. "Barry, man, you know how nobody ever said you weren't a gent?"

He gives me a big grin. "You took that literally?"

I continue to look into there, wherever he is.

He lets himself fall back, out of my grip and onto the couch.

"I guess I'll wait here with Phil, then," he says, laughing good-naturedly.

Phil looks a little desperate, as Barry bites a chicken finger right out of his hand. "Hurry back," he says.

"I hate the bus station," I say. "I really do."

"I don't mind it," she says. "It has its own weird kind of romance to it."

"Speaking of weird romance," I say.

"Listen, Eric. Okay, Barry may not be quite the white knight. But you know what he is? He's a laugh. To be honest, I really, really needed a laugh." She giggles at herself. "I'm not saying I'm proud of myself. And I'm not saying I'd like to spend much more time in his company . . . but, yes, it was good company.

"Duane always gave me a laugh," she says, without laughing.

"Me too," I say. "Well, not *always*."

I go around to the trunk of the car and haul her suitcase out.

"Anyway, I thought your dad took away your car keys," she says.

"He did," I say. "But he always hides them in the same place, the flour canister. Nobody bakes. Where I can find them when I need them. It's that kind of house."

"It is," she says. "Always was."

I'm about to carry the bag inside, but she stops me with a flat, firm palm on my chest. "This is far enough," she says. She throws her arms around my neck, squeezes a kink directly in there, and kisses me eleven times on the cheek in rapid succession. Eleven. Then she looks me in the eyes right up close, her nose lying alongside mine. I feel somebody's tears running over my lips. They taste a little like sugar and a little like monosodium glutamate.

"Take care of yourself, young man," she says.

"Stay," I say.

"No," she says.

"Come back soon," I say.

"No," she says. "I have to live. And I can't do it here. If there is one thing I know in this world . . ."

"Then this is the thing I know," I say.

She grins wickedly, walking backward away from me, towing her wheelie bag.

"Live a little," she says. "Promise me you'll do that, Eric. Have some fun."

I nod at her, a lot. Because that I can do.

She nods back, turns, vanishes.

I must have taken the longest possible way to the bus station, and the longest possible way back. Because it is the wee small hours of the morning, just light, when I reach home.

And find Melinda's car parked out front.

I rush inside, into the living room, where I find Phil asleep on the couch, with Skye the Highland terrier on his hip.

I go to the kitchen, where I find Barry and an empty sangria bottle, and a freshly opened bottle of Irish Mist, which isn't fresh at all since my parents got it for Christmas about twelve years ago.

Barry stands up, goes to a cupboard to get me a glass to share with him.

"Please, by all means make yourself at home," I say.

"You're a great host, I have to tell you, Eric."

"Where are Dean and Melinda?"

"In their room," he says.

I leave him, walk down the hall to Duane's room. I crack the door open to see the two of them curled up together under the stupid, glorious Lord of the Rings bedspread. Melinda half turns over, gives me a small wave over her shoulder, then folds herself again all over the boy.

I close the door gently, ease my way back to the kitchen.

Where I find Barry and his crooked oddball smile sitting at the table, in front of two small glasses of Irish Mist.

"Just this one, then I'm afraid it's time for you to go," I say.
We clink glasses, sip.

"Apparently I need to be more like you," I say.

He looks shocked. "Even I wouldn't recommend that."

"That's actually reassuring," I say.

"This stuff is amazing," he says.

"It's horrendous," I say.

"To Duane," he says.

"To Duane."

Next thing I realize, I have two parents, home from retreat, standing before us.

"A party?" Ma asks.

"A party," Dad says more definitively.

"I'd call it more of a reunion, really," Barry says.

"This is Barry," I say.

Ma would like to know who is on her couch.

"Phil," I say. "And Skye."

"We go away once in . . . well, ever," Dad says, "and you have a party." Shockingly, neither of them seems terribly distressed by this state of affairs. They even look, if it's possible, marginally pleased for me. How sad is that?

"You might not want to look in Duane's room just yet," I say.

Ma looks down the hall in that direction. Dad nods at me. "It's as if an entire alternative life has sprouted up in our absence. Like mushrooms in the basement."

"How was the retreat?" I ask.

Ma pulls her lips really tight, nodding quickly. "Progress," she says. "Better."

"We talked about things," Dad says. "Talked about you, in fact."

"Uh-oh," Barry says. "Drink, anyone?"

"Barry, shut up," I say.

"I'll have one," Dad says, and I'm blown away. I hand him mine.

"We talked about the navy," Ma says, nudging Dad.

He looks at the glass, then at the floor. "You can have your car keys back," he says.

Ma nudges him harder. He shoots down the Irish Mist.

"Stay," Dad says to me.

"Huh?" I say.

"Stay," Ma says.

"Yes," Dad repeats, "stay."

Barry leans over to me. "I think they want you to stay. Unless they mean me. Did you mean me?"

Ma replies, firmly but politely. This is a houseguest, after all. "Uh, no. We mean him."

They mean me.

Stay.

This certainly goes beyond surprising. It goes beyond what the limits of what my admittedly limited imagination could have imagined.

"Well," I say, "I do seem to have torn my hamstring up pretty thoroughly. So I won't be going anywhere. For a while at least."

We seem to have accomplished something, a result. A modest something, but modest somethings are big enough for us around here at this point in history. Without anything more being said, my folks head off to their room, past Duane's room.

"I don't think you ever wanted to go into the stupid navy all along," Barry says.

I get up from the table, head out of the kitchen. "I'm going to bed," I say, and lead him to the door. "Have fun," I say, slapping his back on the way out.

"Don't I always?" he says, and bops off into the sunshine.

Who are these people? Who are they, to me? And who am I, to them? I guess I'm gonna have to work that out now.

I go to the couch, where the dog raises his head, looks at me, then lowers it again. I lean down and whisper into that red ear, into my brother's bones.

"Thanks," I say.

"You're welcome," I hear as I limp my way to Duane's door and listen for a minute. For voices? For soft innocent breathing?

I head to my room, to rest, and to thoughts of the coming day.

The natural history museum, I'm thinking. They will love that.

I will love that.

Live a little.

The problem, or thrill, depending on how you choose to look at it, was that our relationship was practically *based* on an enthusiastic mendacity. Her nickname for me was Lyin' O'Brien. Mine for her was Sweet Junie Blue Lies.

She told me in one of our earliest conversations that her mother had died in a plane crash. And that she had an airplane tattooed on her hip with her mother's initials on the wings. Then I ran into her at CVS four weeks later, where I was cheerfully introduced to her living, earth-walking mother, as well as her sister, Max, who I had been led to believe was her brother, Max. Oh, not an actual plane crash, she said. That was just a metaphor for the marriage. Then after another six long weeks I finally met Junie's hip. There was, in fact, an airplane tattoo. The origin of the initials changed every time I asked. I stopped asking.

Still, thrill is how I choose to look at it. She made lying exciting, and sporty, and really I picked up the habit only when she got me hooked. It was our bond. Then again, we're not together anymore either, so my assessment could be open to question.

June Blue. A guy does not break up with that name lightly. Or voluntarily, as it happens. I was dumped.

She says that her grandfather is a rabbi in London, and I have no reason to doubt her. I told her my grandfather was a bishop in Waterford, and I have no reason not to believe me, either. I've been to his grave, and his headstone is shaped like one of those hats. There you go.

Right? So if that's not soul-matey enough for you, there's our fathers. No, not "Our Fathers," like that moan prayer they used to push in the church, and which would not ever have crossed Junie Blue's puffy orange lips. Our actual fathers. Mine is a robber baron and hers is—whatcha know?—the regular kind. And don't go thinking I mean "baron," all right, since what in the world would a *regular* baron be like?

And they both sell, among other things, insurance.

Before I met him, she told me her father looked exactly like John F. Kennedy. Then I met him. If you dug Kennedy up today, he'd still be better-looking.

Yet in spite of all that, June and I are as honest as the day is long. Unless you count lying, which, really, nobody does.

Honest day's work/honest day's pay, we have no quarrel with that business at all. She works two jobs too, one having grown out of the other, and both legitimate. She works evening and early morning and weekend hours at the corner-store that is about seven corners away from her house. It's in a neighborhood where all corner-store counters would be bulletproof Plexiglassed from the criminals, but for the fact that all their criminals are *their* criminals. And all of *those* criminals are operating under the benevolent eye of One Who Knows, who does not like his neighborhood being dirtied up by petty crime and unwholesomeness that detracts from his sepia view of life in the microclimate that extends four miles in every direction from his modest not-quite-beachside house. You wind up with kneecap and testicle troubles if you screw with One Who Knows and the sepia view.

Junie's humor, right? It's like this. Everybody knows One Who Knows as One Who Knows, except, when we would talk about him, it bothered her to have to sound so, you know, reverential to the guy. Even though she has met him on many occasions and likes him fine enough, she's got her principles still. The guy even has the tattoo down one forearm, the initials stacked like a totem pole, *OWK*. "Owk," Junie said one day, calling me from the store just after he left. He bought a loaf of Wonder Bread and a whole roll of scratch cards and as usual tipped her with ten of those cards. "I mean, thanks for the cards, *Owk*, but, really, *Owk*? It's not even a word or a decent acronym or anything. It's like you asked an owl, 'Hey, what kinda bird are you,' and just when he goes to tell you,

you punch him in the stomach. That's the noise he would make, '*Owk!*'"

I laughed, like I did almost all the time when she talked, but then, also like usual, I began the reasoning process. "So, nobody asked you to call him that. Just use his proper name. One Who Knows."

"Aw, shit to that. I'm not calling anybody that."

"Why not? It's got a ring. Listen," I said, and ran through the full phrasing several different ways, slow and fast and articulated and mumbled and—

"Hold it," she said.

"What?"

"That last one. Do that last one again."

"As I recall," I said, "it went a little something like this . . ."

"That's it," she said.

What I did was rush the three words together, with an opening flourish and a gentle fade-out at the end. Nice work, but nothing special. I do stuff like that all the time.

"Juan Junose." She said the *J*s making *H* sounds, and I could hear her smiling. She has big pearly teeth with a middle gap you could park a cigarette in, which she does sometimes, and it's heart-flutter stuff. Smoking and hearts, eh?

"Juan?" I said.

"From this point onward. Or, Juanward."

I loved the Spanishness of it. Particularly as our Mr.

Junose is the type of guy who, if he found himself being any kind of Spanish, he'd shoot himself in the face.

"Juan," we said at the same time and in the same key. Soul-matey, right?

We did stuff like that regularly, at least until school finished and we unfortunately did likewise. We graduated a month ago, and everything was sailing along like a happy horny boat like always until we hit the reef. I never saw it coming.

"Why?" I asked, and the only reason I didn't sound like a complete weenie dog was because I was taken so entirely by surprise. Given even just a little bit of advance notice, I would have worked up a whimper that would still be singing today if you walked down to the beach and put a seashell to your ear.

I liked June Blue very much. Still do.

"Because we're not kids anymore, O." She liked to call me O, because it fit so well into most of our conversations. *O, for Christsake . . . O, shut up . . . O, God, put that thing away. There are kids in the park. . . .*

"Yes, we are," I said. "Don't let that graduation thing fool you. We're still kids, and will be for quite some time."

She just shook her head at me sadly from her spot so far away at the other end of the seesaw.

"Your head's going in the wrong direction," I said, suddenly bumping the seesaw up and down frantically, getting her whole self into the proper nodding action.

She giggled gloriously but didn't change her mind. She held fast to the seesaw and to the horrible sad squint that was maiming her features. Confusion and panic ran through me like a fast-acting poison, and so, being a clever guy and quick on my feet, I did something.

See, probably the one bone of contention we ever had in a year and a half of going out was that my folks have money, and so I have money, and her family doesn't have anything like that. A problem for her, but I was always cool and magnanimous with it.

So I did something.

"No," she said. "No. You did not."

"What?" I said, removing my hands from the seesaw so I could make the ineffective pleading gesture to the heavens.

"You did *not* just offer me money to stay with you."

Pleading hands were required to stay where they were. "What? No. It wasn't . . . That's not . . . You just misconstrued . . ."

We had the balance thing going pretty well, considering that I outweigh her by about thirty pounds, but when she flung herself backward to get off the seesaw and out of my life, I dropped like a pre-fledgling baby bird to the ground.

And if one of those nestless, flightless, awkward bundles

of patchy feather and hollow bone had been blown up to adult human size and plunked on the ground at the down end of a seesaw, he would not have looked one chirp more ludicrous than I did at that moment.

But I didn't care about that.

"Junie?" I called desperately.

"If you even dare try to follow me, I'll have your legs broken, O."

And since June Blue is one of those rare people who can say that and actually do that and can do it on speed dial, I just sat with my bruised everything until two seesaw-deprived preschool girls came along and stared me into slouching away home.

Her second job is dog walker. Visitors to the store started asking after she took care of the owner's mutt for a couple of days when he had a couple of toes excommunicated because of diabetes. People in June's neighborhood apparently have diabetes at such a rate that people get toes popped like having bad teeth removed, and word spreads fast when there is a reliable babysitter, window washer, or dog walker around. June is popular, and busy, and one of her sometimes clients is the man himself, Juan, who has the ugliest Boston terrier on earth, with three deep scars across his snout and an ass like a tiny little baboon.

I take walks sometimes. It's not stalking.

I don't take binoculars, or rope, or flowers.

I take hope, best intentions, and, okay, that spicy ginger chewing gum that she loves and you can only get in Chinatown, but that hardly changes anything.

"That tree isn't even wider than you, doofus," she says.

What does one do in this situation? I'm looking a little simple here, skinnying myself behind this immature beech tree diagonally across from the house that June has just stepped out of. I'm not stupid. I know this tree is not adequate for my purpose, but I had my eye on a burly elm only fifteen yards farther, when June and that Airedale with the bad nature stepped out the door a full ten minutes before the usual walking time for a Tuesday.

"I'm not stalking you," I say, still inexplicably remaining there, only partially obscured by the sapling. I may have lost my fastball, lying-wise.

She continues on her appointed round.

"Stalking Archie, then?"

"He's not my type."

"Good. 'Cause he doesn't like you either."

It's true, he doesn't, but more important, what did she mean by that, "doesn't like you, either"? *Either* as in, Archie and I share a mutual animosity? Or she and Archie share a dislike of me? This is the kind of stupid, obsessive thought

I have now? Look what you've done to me, Junie Blue.

"Did you just say you didn't like me?" I say pathetically as she strides down the block and away from me again.

"No," she says. And that's all she says.

"Gum?" I call after her, the pack held aloft like I am the Statue of Liberty's tiny little embarrassing brother.

The high school we went to is often cited in lists as America's finest public school. There is a citywide exam to get in after sixth grade, and I was determined to take it even though the highly rated private school I went to had everything but its own moat. I alarmed my parents both by doing well on the exam and by insisting on going there. Rebellion? No. I'm pretty sure I was intent on meeting a greater variety of girl-folk. There were no Junie Blues in my previous existence, that's for sure.

When June and I were still students there, things were much better. We had two classes together final term, and I tell you what, in those classes I did not learn a money-humping thing.

English and history, and we clung like mutual barnacles to each other's hull for every class, making jokes and talking all manner of nonsense. We had our regular seats, and we would always make plans to meet there, as if there were any mystery at all as to where we were going to sit.

"Back of English," she would say, pointing at me as we

passed in the corridor prior to third period Tuesday and Thursday.

"Wrong side of history," I would say prior to fourth period Wednesday and Friday. It was a favorite term of our history teacher, Mr. Lyons, whom everybody called Jake, and who talked with this fantastic squelch effect like he had a tracheotomy. *You don't want to wind up on the wrong side of history*, Jake would say whenever he was pointing out some of the greatest errors in judgment that hindsight could illuminate. I always thought hindsight gave history teachers the most lopsided advantage over pretty much everybody they ever talked about, but Jake was rather modest in his infallibility just the same.

In more practical terms the wrong side of our history was in the southwest corner of the room, where the window was drafty and the overhead light flickered like in a disco. I sat behind June and rubbed her shoulders when the wind blew, and that buzzing overhead fluorescent was a kind of sound track to our little wrong-side romance. Bzzzz.

The point, though, was that the back of English, the wrong side of history, wherever we were in May was a better place than where we were just a few weeks later, and I am none the wiser still as to why.

Bad overhead lighting makes me melancholy now.

Transcending stories of life-changing friendship from Benjamin Alire Sáenz

★ "The protagonists and their friends seem so real and earn the audience's loyalty so legitimately that it will be hard for readers to part with them."
—*Publishers Weekly*, starred review, on *He Forgot to Say Goodbye*

★ "Meticulous pacing and finely nuanced characters underpin the author's gift for affecting prose that illuminates the struggles within relationships."
—*Kirkus Reviews*, starred review, on *Aristotle and Dante Discover the Secrets of the Universe*